PRAISE FOR CORIN

LIBERATION: nominated for 1
ELFLING: 1st prize, Teen Fiction, CPA ~~Book~~
I AM MARGARET & *BANE'S EYES:* finalists, *CALA Award 2016/2018.*
LIBERATION & *THE SIEGE OF REGINALD HILL:* 3rd place, *CPA Book Awards 2016/2019.*

Corinna Turner was awarded the **St. Katherine Drexel Award** in **2022.**

PRAISE FOR *ELFLING*

I was instantly drawn in

EOIN COLFER, author of *Artemis Fowl* and former Children's Laureate of Ireland.

PRAISE FOR *A RIGHT REX RODEO*

I've long been curious about what sparked Corinna Turner's imagination to somehow think of writing a series that combines faith, action, and dinosaurs. Whatever ignited her creativity, the result is the raptorously fantastic unSPARKed series. The short episodic formula used in these books brilliantly unfolds the story in quick, fast-paced segments.
In A Right Rex Rodeo, *Darryl and Harry continue the search for their father with dino-hunter Josh. I'm always impressed with the fictional worlds that Corinna Turner creates. This particular book is full of these Turner-esque details as the teens take a little time out of their roaming to attend a rodeo—not just any rodeo—a dinosaur rodeo. While I loved the fascinating in-depth look into the dino-hunter world, the edge-of-your-seat action kept me turning the pages.*

Beware: this series' vivid descriptions, heart-pounding drama, and fabulous characters are sure to lure you in, as well.
LESLEA WAHL, author of the Blindside series

A Right Rex Rodeo *is a satisfying next installment in the series, with a rodeo, lots of dinosaurs and other dangers, and more details about the fascinating dino-hunter culture Corinna Turner has created.*
MARIE C. KEISER, author of *Heaven's Hunter*

ALSO BY CORINNA TURNER:

I AM MARGARET series
For older teens and up

Brothers *(A Prequel Novella)**
1: I Am Margaret*
1: Io Sono Margaret (Italian)
2: The Three Most Wanted*
3: Liberation*
4: Bane's Eyes*
5: Margo's Diary*
6: The Siege of Reginald Hill*
7: A Saint in the Family
'The Underappreciated Virtues of Rusty Old Bicycles' *(Prequel short story) Also found in the anthology:*
Secrets: Visible & Invisible*

I Am Margaret: The Play *(Adapted by Fiorella de Maria)*

UNSPARKED series
For tweens and up

Main Series:
1: Please Don't Feed the Dinosaurs
2: A Truly Raptor-ous Welcome
3: PANIC!*
4: Farmgirls Die in Cages*
5: Wild Life
6: A Right Rex Rodeo
7: FEAR†

Prequels:
BREACH!*
A Mom With Blue Feathers†
A Very Jurassic Christmas*
'Liam and the Hunters of Lee'Vi'

FRIENDS IN HIGH PLACES series
For tweens and up

1: The Boy Who Knew (Carlo Acutis)*
2: Old Men Don't Walk to Egypt (Saint Joseph)*
3: Child, Unwanted (Margaret of Castello)

Do Carpenter's Dream of Wooden Sheep? *(Spin-off, comes between 1 & 2)*

1: El Chico Que Lo Sabia (Spanish)
1: Il Ragazzo Che Sapeva (Italian)

YESTERDAY & TOMORROW series
For adults and mature teens only
Someday: A Novella*
Eines Tages (German)
1: Tomorrow's Dead†

OTHER WORKS

For teens and up
Elfling*
'The Most Expensive Alley Cat in London'
(Elfling prequel short story)

For tweens and up
Mandy Lamb & The Full Moon*
The Wolf, The Lamb, and The Air Balloon
(Mandy Lamb novella)

For adults and new adults
Three Last Things *or* The Hounding of Carl Jarrold, Soulless Assassin*
A Changing of the Guard

The Raven & The Yew†

† **Coming Soon**
* **Awarded the Catholic Writers Guild** *Seal of Approval*

6

A RIGHT
REX RODEO

CORINNA TURNER

unSeen

CONTENTS

DARRYL

If only we'd had some hint of...of *anything* concerning Dad. Who took him. Where he is. Even simply whether he's still alive. If they catch us before we've rescued him...ransomed him...whichever...Josh will go to prison for *nothing*.

But we've no leads. Not a *thing*. Ow, I'm tugging my long brown braid far too hard. Stupid. As Dad would say: *Darryl, my girl, that won't help a rat's tail.* We can't do anything we're not already doing, and that's that. Even if all we're doing is staying free and letting Josh's friends keep their ears open.

The more I learn about hunter economics the more I appreciate what Josh is giving up for us. Hunters are obsessed with saving—saving for expensive repairs to their habitat vehicles, for replacement gear, saving for that dreaded day when they need a whole new HabVi and, even, like Technicolor 'Vi, saving for that long-dreamt-of time when they can own their own camp. But, thanks to our fugitive status, the Wilson HabVi has been running at subsistence level for months; no savings for Josh. He feels so like family now it doesn't seem strange that he thinks helping us is worth it, but we sure are grateful.

Summer is long gone. Well, not really. But Harry and I grew up in the snug Franklyn farmhouse and, living in the Wilson habitat vehicle, you really feel the difference. For my seventeenth birthday in August we met up with Technicolor HabVi to have a cook-out with West, Thiago, and Ed in blazing sunshine.

September came, and the nights turned cold. For Josh's nineteenth birthday last week, we ate inside, with rain hammering on the metal roof. Now we're dodging mud deep enough to get bogged in, as well as staying away from anywhere Highway Patrol might roam.

Josh did keep telling me and Harry that summer was the comfy season. This winter could be long and hard, considering how little contact we're able to have with anyone else. The Child Protective Services are *still* after Darryl and Harry Franklyn, can you believe, even after all these months? I'd admire Fernanda Matthews' perseverance if she wasn't trying to ruin our lives and get our dad killed. She's determined to lock up Harry and me in-city because we're 'too young' to be working out here for Josh.

2

The 'Vi heaves over the pass, the pivoting double rear axles handling the sharp ridge effortlessly, and then our nose is pointing downhill again after two hours of uphill climbing.

"When are you gonna teach me to drive this thing?" Harry asks Josh.

"*Going to,*" I mutter. Heck, by the time we find Dad, Harry's going to be speaking fluent Hunter.

"Josh says *gonna.*"

"Josh is a hunter. That's what hunters say."

"We're hunters now."

"Temporarily."

Harry snorts. Josh takes his brown eyes from the slope to flick me a searching look—oh no, have I offended him?—but after a second he just gives me an understanding smile. Phew.

It's not that I don't like hunting. Actually, I'm kinda loving this life. But acting like—accepting that—we *are* hunters now, not farmers, feels like giving up on ever saving Dad. I'm not ready to do that. At least Josh gets it.

"You've let Darryl drive twice," Harry persists.

"He gave me two *lessons*—and on better terrain than this, Harry." I jerk my head down the craggy slope.

"I don't mean right *now.* But if driving the 'Vi really is so very different than a tractor or farm truck, shouldn't I know for...for emergencies?" Harry keeps the whine from his voice—he's very good at acting

3

grown-up now and avoiding disapproving looks from Josh—but I know he's just coming up with any reason he can think of. We spent Harry's fourteenth birthday in June hiding in a canyon under heavy camouflage while helicopters quartered the area for three days. Josh reckoned it was military training and nothing to do with us—but we hid anyway.

Josh nods seriously in response to Harry's question, the faint curl in his untidy black hair making it bounce. Any day now he's going to ask me to cut it before it gets in his gun sight—and I'd better do Harry's, too. "It is," he replies. "And you're right, it's time I trained you both. No crisis is improved by rolling the 'Vi belly-up, that's for sure."

Rolling the 'Vi belly up *is* a crisis—there's a whole procedure Josh has taught us to deal with it. But shock, delight, and triumph dart over my little brother's face as he grins at me. I can't help smiling in return.

"And get ready for handicraft making," adds Josh, with a sly grin at Harry, who is known not to be looking forward to this. "'Tis the season."

Harry rolls his green eyes but is clearly too excited about the driving to care.

The season...will we spend Christmas in the 'Vi? Without Dad? Birthdays without him were weird enough.

"You should be keen to practice your crafts," Josh adds, "then you can enter the competitions at the

Midwinter Fair. Though..." His face falls. "I guess we won't go to that this year."

Despite Josh's last words, Harry's face lights up with interest. He opens his mouth—just as Josh stamps on the brakes so hard that we're all flung forward against our chest harnesses, which Josh is very firm about keeping on in this mountainous terrain. Kiko screeches, half-falling, half-fluttering from my shoulder onto the dashboard in a flurry of wing-limbs but landing unhurt.

"Josh?"

Shoulders tense, his eyes fixed on something in the valley far, far below, Josh backs up until we're behind a crag, then cuts the engine.

"*Misfire*, did they see us?" he mutters, then snaps, "Get up the turret and cover me!"

With that, he opens the driver's door and leaps out.

"Josh?" I yelp, horrified. Okay, we've been keeping our eyes open, quartering our surroundings, as we drive, but we haven't checked properly for danger.

Flat on the ground, he crawls forward to peer around the crag, down into the valley. "Just cover me!" he snarls into his ScreamerBand. "We've gotta know if they saw us!"

I'm already grabbing my rifle from beside the seat and dashing up to the turret, raising the windows. Heck, this is a terrible spot to go out-Vi, tucked down between rocky outcrops like this. There's cover for

5

critters to creep up all around. I reach for the drone controls, then hesitate.

"And *don't* launch the drone!" Josh's voice comes from my ScreamerBand again. "They might see it."

"What the *short-circuiting fences* is going on?" says Harry, as the two of us take half each and keep the best watch we can with such a limited field of vision. At least there are unlikely to be any large carni'saurs this high up, but a pair of deinons or a pack of velociraptors are a big threat to one person.

"Language, Harry," I chide, half-heartedly since Josh just swore too. "Clearly there's something dangerous down there and Josh doesn't want to take his eyes off it."

"What is it?"

I shrug. Probably some*one*, not some*thing*, but there can't possibly be a highway patrol vehicle way out here and, anyway, Josh has never reacted this badly to one. There's nothing more to say until Josh finally gets to his feet and returns to the 'Vi.

"Let's move!" His voice comes over the intercom, the huge vehicle shifting fractionally as he settles back into the driver's seat. "Stay up there and keep your eyes open."

"*Was* it Highway Patrol?" demands Harry.

"Worse. Jason and Co."

"Jason Desmoines?" I check. The guy has come up a few times in Josh's stories. He sounds like a real dud egg with a nasty grudge against the Wilson family, of which Josh is the last surviving member.

"Yeah. But I only saw *his* 'Vi and he hunts in a pair with one of his cousins, usually. So let me know immediately if you see any sign of another HabVi. Jason might've deliberately headed straight on to fool us into thinking he didn't see us, while sending Masey around to circle behind us."

I picture the mountain we've just climbed and glance at the terrain ahead, visible on the map on the console screen. "That'd be one big circle."

"Yeah, so if we don't hang around, we should be gone before they get here. And I sure ain't hanging around." The 'Vi moves forward even as he speaks, and I catch the rail to steady myself.

"Is Jason really that dangerous?" It didn't sound like things had gone beyond taunts and snide remarks at the 'Vi-park.

"Not normally, but Jason ain't nice people and Uncle Z punched some of his teeth out once, which he ain't never forgiven. The authorities want me for supposedly kidnapping you two, right? So if Jason shows up in-city the hero with you two and regretfully informs the police that I got shot dead during the 'rescue,' d'you think anyone will give a rat's tail? Between the two 'Vis, there's seven of them and only one of me. Could be the easiest revenge they ever took in their lives."

"There's *three* of us," I say.

"I ain't letting Jason anywhere near you or Harry if I can help it." He hesitates, then adds, "He...he just...*ain't nice*, okay?"

Ain't nice to *women*, I guess that means? Huh. Josh is very innocent about women in many ways—I'm guessing he's barely known any, not really well—but some things he is alert to. This Jason guy just gets better and better.

"Anyway, we need to scoot," says Josh. "At the very least he could dump the police on us the moment he gets satellite lock."

"That's, like, totally against hunter rules, though, isn't it?" protests Harry.

"Only if you're at a fair, then the Peace of the Fair holds. Otherwise, it ain't the done thing but it ain't actually forbidden, not if someone's *actually* done something illegal."

I exchange a look with Harry. Problem is, according to Father Ben, Josh *has* done something illegal by rescuing us from Fernanda Matthews and the city— though he didn't mean to and most hunters wouldn't care.

"I wonder what he's doing all the way up here?" Josh muses as he drives. "It's not his kinda hunting patch. He sticks to easy terrain and easy kills."

"Could it be to do with Dad?" Harry asks eagerly.

Josh sighs. "No reason to think that, especially after

all these months. Jason's rotten enough, sure, but so are plenty of other guys."

Three days later, we're at the opposite end of Exception State—with no sign of pursuit. Jason didn't see us—or he was too busy doing what he was doing to bother about us. Which means, Josh says dryly, knowing how Jason feels about the Wilson HabVi—that he probably didn't see us.

HARRY

I poke at the leather with an awl, making yet another hole for yet another tooth. Handicraft making is as boring as I feared, though Darryl's really into it. Right now she's showing Josh the belt she just finished. He likes the design, predictably.

After sighing over my early efforts, he drew out a pattern for me to reproduce on a belt in teeth and beads. Which is easier than trying to be 'creative.'

The wind howls, shaking the 'Vi from side to side, even with the stabilizers down. It's broad daylight and there's no fresh snow today, but the gale is so violent we're sitting tight. We're still high in a mountainous region, despite it being winter, when most hunters stick to warmer altitudes. Being wanted stinks. Back at the farm, further south and lower down, we'd just be getting snow occasionally and enjoying the novelty rather than sitting around indoors bundled up in multiple layers.

Lent has started, too—oh boy, has it started! But we've agreed there's no point trying to tell anyone other than Father Ben about that insane Ash Wednesday—not even West and the others. They'll never believe us!

It turns out most hunter-borns keep Lent strictly, even if they're not that well catechized. Josh hasn't cooked any cakes or desserts since Shrove Tuesday, and when it was my turn to cook and I reached for the spices he looked so shocked I couldn't bring myself to put any in, though I missed them already. It's a dull season, all right.

Kiko grabs a tooth from the pot in front of me and retreats, chewing on it.

"You can't eat that," I tell him, but he carries on gnawing. Bored too. Everyone's working and not giving him attention. I'd give him some but I don't want to be the slacker. West, Thiago, and Ed—who're like uncles to Josh—still meet us every month or so for re-supply, whatever the weather, but it has to be paid for. With that wind howling, I don't even *want* to slack.

I poke another hole with the awl.

It was a quiet Christmas, just the three of us—and Kiko—in the 'Vi, tucked away in some sheltered valley out in the deep wilderness. No carol service. No Mass. No Dad. And, of course, all we had to give each other were handicraft items. Still, I love the ammo pouches Josh gave me, with their rugged claw and tooth decoration. I like owning the stuff, just not making it!

Ed went to West and Thiago's home camp with them for Christmas, apparently. Or rather, the camp they grew up at. Their fathers both worked for the guys who own it. Thiago's dad died but West's is retired and still lives there with his mother, along with Thiago's mum. There's no space for either West or Thiago to set up home there, though.

Ed did have a proper home camp, apparently, but he allowed his brother to buy out his share after he took along a young jackal he'd raised from a pup and his brother shot it on sight because his wife had a new baby—without giving Ed a chance to simply take it away. Ed's always picking up injured or orphaned critters to care for so that was the moment he knew he'd never want to live there again, full-time.

We met with Technicolor for New Year's and had a lively evening drinking ginger ale while West lit a barbeque up in their turret and kept the charred meat coming on soft, city-bought bread rolls. Thiago didn't even complain about helping us, all evening, not once— he's been getting less and less happy about the risk they're running. West's not really that happy about it, either. Setting up their own camp has taken on a whole new urgency—West started courting some pretty widow back in the summer and is now desperate to be able to "offer her a fence."

We gave them the nicest belated Christmas gifts we

could make, you bet we did! Without them, we'd have had to leave the state and give up any hope of saving Dad.

Dad. My heart sinks. Still no news. Nothing via Father Ben, either, though we've seen him a couple of times, very briefly so no one notices any delay in his journey. I don't even want to let the thought in my head, but it's getting harder and harder to deny that Dad's probably dead.

It's almost March, now, and the 'Midwinter' Fair's coming up in less than a week—it takes place across Saint Desmond's Day, nowadays. Josh told Technicolor we weren't going when we parted at New Year, but I haven't seen anyone except the same six people for *almost a year* and after several months of handicrafting with limited outdoor work, that fair is starting to look sooooooo good.

"I wish we *could* go." The words pop out, before I can help myself. "I mean, if no one's *allowed* to turn anyone in..."

Josh, busy stitching a large claw to a pouch of some kind, shoots me a look and sighs. "I know how you feel, Harry. But there's no point us risking it. It's better to just lie low."

I open my mouth again but Darryl fixes me with a glare. Yeah, okay. If we get caught I'm 'only' going to a foster home. She's going to juvie and Josh, who, in city-folk's eyes, committed the unforgiveable sin of taking us in despite already being eighteen...poor Josh goes to prison. I'm asking him to risk that, for some fun and games?

I close my mouth. Then change the subject. "West sure does talk about Trudi Harman a lot. How do Thiago and Ed bear it?"

Josh and Darryl laugh.

"Honestly," says Josh, "I think he talks about her more to us. We're fresh ears."

"Yeah, and in our position we can hardly threaten to shoot him if he doesn't shut up."

That makes them both laugh some more, though they sober up quickly.

Yeah, West wants his Trudi to go with them when they start viewing derelict smallholdings, be involved as they choose the right one to purchase for their long-dreamt-of camp, but apparently in the Hunter-verse the invitation would be downright offensive unless he's already popped the question. Which he seems reluctant to do while conspiring with fugitives.

Yep, we're really starting to disrupt West's love-life and all of Technicolor's life plans, big time, which doesn't make us feel good. And if Dad is...gone...then Josh is the only family Darryl and I have. Maybe we *should* leave Exception state before the city-folk can split us up. Another state won't be so interested in us. We could go to fairs, resupply in-city ourselves, live a normal hunter life.

But Father Ben said crossing state boundaries would make things worse for Josh in the eyes of the law. And it would mean giving up on Dad *entirely*. We can't do that. Not yet.

Not yet? Then when? Never, right? We don't need to. If Darryl does get custody of me, we can go back to the farm and we'll be right there for kidnappers to contact. But it's odd to think of living there, without Dad. Without Josh? He was only gonna come and help us out for a time. I miss the farm—I reckon I want to be a farmer, not a hunter, long-term—yet right now it hardly feels real. Real life is here, in the 'Vi, out in the wind and the wilderness. *And* Darryl's birthday is another six months away. Six more months of needing Technicolor's help.

Six more months in which to get caught...

JOSHUA

I zip my parka right up to my chin and pick up my steaming mug, wrapping my gloved hands around its warmth. The sun scatters pink and gold rays over the mist as it rises, framing the mountains behind it. I've always been an early riser, like my dad, not that rising with the sun means rising that early, at this time of year.

Soon soft sounds from below and slight movements of the vehicle tell me that Darryl is up. Harry's more like Uncle Z, prone to sleeping in unless there's a reason

14

to turn out quickly, which there rarely is in winter.

I know Darryl's finished her oatmeal when she opens the hatch and Kiko suddenly swoops ahead of her into the turret. I stroke him as she climbs up with her own coffee. If it was Harry, I'd tell him to shut the hatch again to keep the heat in down below. But it's Darryl, so I don't and she doesn't. I'm guessing farmer rules and hunter rules about doors and whether or not you're actually blood-related are pretty similar. She looks so womanly nowadays, sometimes I catch myself noticing, though I try not to. I mean, I'm the boss, she's only seventeen, and her dad's nowhere to be found.

She looks real serious, this morning, as she settles into a chair on the opposite side of the turret and stares out at the dawn. I don't say nothing. If there's something on her mind, she'll spit it out when she's ready.

"The fair, Josh," she says at last, when she's drunk most of her rapidly cooling coffee. "How dangerous *would* it be for us to go?"

I sit up and give her my full attention. The fair? That's what's on her mind?

"Well, not *very*. Siting it in a blind alley so no one can get a satellite connection is an old tradition and it makes everyone feel safe to come, gives 'The Peace of the Fair' teeth, y'know? To turn someone in at a fair, you'd have to leave early and, trust me, you can't do that without *everyone* knowing."

"So if someone left early, we could leave immediately? How risky then?"

"Not very at all. It just seems unnecessary." Don't get me wrong, I love the fair, but when I think about *prison*...locked up, *in-city*, for who knows how long... Just the thought brings me out in a cold sweat. Nope, I'm not even slightly tempted.

Darryl nods. "Yeah, I was all for not risking it, but I've been thinking about Dad. We have *no leads*. It's been almost a year since he disappeared. How long will someone keep him, Josh?"

I wince, which is answer enough for her.

She nods again and goes on, "If someone *does* still have him, maybe, just maybe, they simply haven't worked out how to contact us. This fair is the largest in three states, you said?"

I nod. Hunters from Tana, Exception, and Yoming will all gather.

"So the kidnappers might *be there*. And if they're not, it's our best chance of hearing *something*. I feel like...like this could be our last chance to help Dad." She stares at me solemnly with her blue eyes.

"So you want to go?"

"It has to be up to you. But as far as Dad is concerned, doesn't it make sense?"

I lean back in my chair, staring up at the turret ceiling, turning her words in my mind. She's right. This really could be our last chance. If they ever catch me...

It'd be nice to have actually saved William Franklyn, since I'll be going to prison either way.

I clench my fists as my breathing speeds up, ice creeping up my spine at the very thought. I will *not* go to prison. I will run, I will hide, I will...I'm not going.

I push that from my mind. "Okay. Wake Harry. If we're going to the fair, we've a long way to travel and we need to hit the road."

DARRYL

As Harry eases the 'Vi carefully through the pass, the fairground is suddenly visible below. A flat valley, surrounded by a mountain chain, in a wild-enough region to keep city-folk away, though more accessible than the places we've been lurking recently.

There are still gaps, but a great ring of Habitat Vehicles already encircles a large central area. We've made it before the fair officially starts, but we're not exactly early birds after our last minute decision to come.

Harry sits straight and proud in the driver's seat, staring eagerly down into the valley as he eases the 'Vi to a halt. I pull the binoculars from the door pouch and focus, trying to hold down my own excitement. We're here to find Dad, not just for fun. I can make out arenas, different areas, stalls... I've no idea what half of it is for. A few people are working on setting things up but

17

other than that it's deserted, despite all the vehicles already present.

Josh unhooks the high-powered telescopic sight from his rifle, scrutinizing the fairground even more closely. Or rather, the entrances.

"Okay, there's Trudi on the nearest gate. She knows me; we'll go in there. Uh," he glances at Harry, "no offence, but I'm gonna drive now."

"*West's* Trudi?" I ask, as Harry yields the wheel to him with a good grace, probably no keener than Josh for our 'Vi to come to grief in front of the largest audience of hunters you could easily find gathered anywhere.

"Well, he's sure hoping so," grins Josh. "Widow her age, she could take her pick. My dad and Uncle Z would've been lining up, I bet."

"But she likes him, right?" I check.

"Oh, sure, from what Thiago and Ed say, she wants him, all right. If he don't drag his feet too long. Funny how quickly West dropped the idea of equal shares in their camp once Trudi came along."

"Ed can put up half the funds, right, and West and Thiago a quarter each?" says Harry. "Meaning they can get on and look for somewhere right away? That's what he was telling me at New Year. But that will make Ed camp boss even though West is boss of the 'Vi?"

"Yeah. They were gonna wait, go for a straight three-way split. Which is generally considered preferable when the 'Vi is already unequal shares—

18

unless it's the same shares as the 'Vi, anyway. But other arrangements work, for people who've co-owned together long enough. Ed could've bought more than a quarter share of a 'Vi, y'know, but he took what was available in Technicolor precisely because he got on with West and Thiago and they're prepared to tolerate his endless procession of small furry critters—more or less. They do make him offload them to a petting farm now and then, when they get too big or too many."

Harry laughs. I murmur, "Fair enough." You really can't keep many animals in a 'Vi, long-term. Not that I can talk, since I have Kiko, but he's very well behaved.

Josh loves all critters, 'saur or mammal, but his Uncle Z was more of the mindset of Ed's brother about animals so Josh has had to make do with transient critter friends on route to zoos, mostly. He's not as sentimental as Ed about small, furry animals, that's for sure. Current score since we've been with him: one rabbit with a broken leg, splinted and released, a pretty river squirrel splinted and sold to a petting zoo, and another injured rabbit cooked for dinner because he said he'd been fancying rabbit all day and he wasn't going to look Saint Des's gift in the mouth.

It's another half-hour before we're down on the valley floor, approaching the closest place where vehicles are entering the site, marked by nothing other than a pair of wooden posts on each side of where two muddy lines of wheelmarks mar the snow. A woman gripping a handPad, a rifle over her shoulder, stands there, speaking to each vehicle, noting things down, and pointing them onwards. I don't see a fence around the site, though hunters are visible in some of the turrets with unmirrored windows, clearly keeping watch.

The woman's eyebrows go up as we roll towards her. She's got very deep black skin, even darker than West's, and her hair's up in thin braids, fastened around her head in a coronet shape with lots of colored leather cords.

"Huh, she *is* pretty," says Harry.

"Sure is," agrees Josh.

Seriously? Oh dear, why does their admiration bother me? She *is* very pretty, despite being Carol's age. Guess I'm not used to my little brother noticing women; that must be it.

I'm more curious about her clothes. I already know she's a 'huntress'—a hunter woman who actually hunts—currently working in an uncle's 'Vi, so it's no surprise that she's wearing the same sort of everyday hunter gear as Josh, heavy cotton camo and a good quality parka. But she also has a sleeveless leather waistcoat—heavily decorated, hunter-style—over the top, falling to mid-thigh. Is that, like, fancy female wear? Fancy activewear?

Rather than merely dropping a high-up window, Josh politely opens the cab door so she can see in properly. "Hi, Trudi."

"Joshua Wilson, I weren't expecting to see you here this year."

Joshua shrugs. "Peace of the Fair."

Trudi moves so she can peer past him at Harry and me. I smile; Harry grins like an over-excited child, though his winter-pale cheeks go red under her scrutiny. "So, uh, you two been kidnapped?" she inquires.

I roll my eyes, so does Harry. We chorus, "No."

"Didn't think so. Not really Joshua's way." She shoots Josh a look. "Well, she is pretty, for a farmgirl. You should've married her, though; you'll make Saint Des mad."

My cheeks heat up as Josh's warm brown skin tone darkens with embarrassment.

"It's not like *that*, neither," he says firmly.

"If you say so. Go on and join the ring, then."

"I was hoping you might need a gatepost."

She shoots him a sharp look. "Huh. Yeah, figures. Okay, we're ready for one here." She points to the side of the entrance. "I'll guide you in."

With Trudi waving her arms occasionally but not needing to do much, Josh backs the 'Vi very precisely into position in line with the other HabVis, until we're virtually touching the front of the vehicle behind, our nose level with the wooden post that marks the gateway. When he cuts off the engine, Trudi gives him a thumbs-up and moves to speak to the next arrival.

I eye the vehicles in the 'ring,' all parked so nose-to-tail that I don't see how one could wriggle out without about twenty or thirty vehicles inching along to free up space, and something clicks. "So, we want to be a 'gatepost' so we can leave quickly if we need to, right?"

Josh nods and grins. "That's right. Anyone *can* leave early—but 'breaking the ring' puts so many people to trouble that you don't do it lightly and everyone will know. If a gatepost leaves, we'll know, too. Gossip is lightning-fast at an event like this."

"Can we go out and see everything?" asks Harry eagerly.

Josh laughs. "Not yet. Fair hasn't started yet. At least one of us needs to get up top and keep watch. Wouldn't want anything to eat Trudi and the other organizers, would you?"

All three of us go up, of course, Harry and I peering around at everything while Josh actually keeps his eyes open for danger.

"So the HabVis *are* the fence?" I say.

"Yeah, but there's a big gap under each of 'em, of course, so a fairground ain't as secure as a camp or farm, right? So we take our rifles with us in case of a breach. Not likely, though. This many humans puts off even the largest carni'saurs, if they've any experience at all."

And if any brash juvenile rex or allo barges into a gathering like this, it won't live long enough to do much damage, I bet.

"When will it start?" asks Harry.

Josh looks bemused. "When the ring is complete."
He doesn't add 'of course' but we can hear it.

Vehicles are arriving thick and fast, so hopefully it
won't be long. Oh dear, I'm almost as eager as Harry!
Hunter fairs are near-mythical among farmers. I don't
know anyone who's actually been to one. Would they
even let farmers in?

"Darryl, can you take the watch for a minute?" says
Josh, rising to go below.

"Sure." I sit down and fix my eyes determinedly on
the landscape. I'm a grown-up hunter...farmgirl...
whichever, right? I can concentrate. I can't believe Trudi
thought Josh should've *married* me, though. I'm only
seventeen! I s'pose that *is* old enough, legally, if Dad
okayed it. But Dad isn't here and like Josh said, it's not
like that! I try to push it from my mind, staring out, my
eyes checking around bushes and boulders.

As soon as Josh has closed the hatch behind him...
"I can't believe that woman thought Josh should *marry*
you," says Harry.

So much for forgetting about it! My cheeks heat up
again.

"Clearly hunters think it's better to marry than sin,"
I say, trying to sound totally calm and casual. "I guess
they're not wrong about that."

"But you're not sinning."

23

"Which is why we ain't getting married, oddly enough!"

"*Are not*," smirks Harry.

"Yeah, yeah." My cheeks heat up even more.

Harry starts focusing the binos on another part of the fair and seems to forget the subject, so I try to do the same. It is weird, though, to think that in only another six months time I could marry someone *without* Dad's permission. Despite how important eighteen has been looming in my life for the last year, I've never really thought about *that* aspect of it.

HARRY

There's so much of the fairground to look at with the binos, but I still keep thinking about what Trudi said. The thought of anyone *marrying* my big sister is...horrifying. But still, the more I think about it...Josh... Wouldn't be so bad, I guess. If she *had* to marry *someone*. I mean, no one could say we weren't a family and tear us apart then, could they?

The sun is dropping in the sky and the flow of vehicles slowing as Josh steps back up into the turret. He's put on the fancy leg wear he showed us the other day, like chaps but instead of a leather fringe there's a massive line of multi-colored raptor feathers down each edge, sticking out to the side. The effect is pretty spectacular, though he says it's nothing compared to

24

what guys from camps will have on.

"Vi-dwellers can't keep full traditional outfits," he told us. "No space to store much that ain't good for out-Vi work. Leather smells so strong—and tasty—and you can't clean it easy. Get blood on it and you'd be best to throw it away, pronto. Hunters used to rub things like stink-root into it, in the early days, when they wanted that leather gear for extra protection. Oddly enough, washable cotton is more popular for daily wear nowadays!"

We had to drive from dawn to dusk to get here, so Darryl and I didn't have time to make anything like his chaps, but Josh did fish out his Uncle Z's fur hood for me and his own old one for Darryl. He wears his dad's at fairs now, apparently. He gave Darryl some white rabbit fur to trim it with and advice on how to quickly alter the bead and feather work to make it pass for a lady's hood—which she had just enough time in the evenings to get done.

He told us not to worry about having no chaps. Apparently it's hunter tradition to make all formal gear yourself and city-borns often can't be bothered. So I'm going to look like a city-born—*great*.

"Here, these are for you two," Josh says, holding out two cash cards. "I loaded 'em with some of the wages I'm keeping for you."

"Awesome!" I accept the card eagerly. We're at the fair *and* we have spending money!

"We're staying together, mind you," says Josh firmly. "We can't make a quick getaway if one of us has wandered off somewhere, and you two ain't exactly familiar with this kind of thing."

"Can't be that different from a country rodeo, right?" I say, as Darryl smiles a thank you and accepts her card, tucking it quickly away without taking her eyes from the landscape for long.

"Oh, there'll be rodeo alright," grins Josh, "and there ain't no rodeo like hunter rodeo."

I'm going to ask more, but then a 'Vi engine starts up nearby. It's the vehicle that's been parked nearby, but not part of the ring. And it's...yes, it's moving out through the gateway, turning sideways, reversing into position, overlapping with both 'gateposts' to close the gateway!

Our gate is sealed. I try not to bounce from foot to foot. It must be almost time!

"Hey!" I peer down. "That guy is *writing* on us!"

"Relax, it's just the watch schedule. Why don't you go see what we've got?"

Got?

I slide down the ladder and open the side door, leaning out to read what's just been chalked on the side of the 'Vi. "Two AM," I call up the turret. "Seven AM. Three PM."

"One-hour slots," says Josh, once I'm back in the turret. "I'll take two AM. Darryl, you take seven in the

26

morning. Harry, you'll be three in the afternoon."

"Aw," I groan. "Why does Darryl get seven AM? I'll miss way more fun stuff in the afternoon."

Josh gives me the look that says I've just complained about something a hunter-born wouldn't have but speaks patiently. "Darryl's more naturally alert at seven AM than you are. So she takes seven, and you get three."

And Josh gets two AM because the night watch is the hardest and he's the most experienced? I guess at an event like this, security trumps pleasure every time. And, thinking about it, he and Darryl will be doing two watches each and me only one. If only I'd just nodded and accepted my watch without moaning about it! When will I learn? Still, I don't open my big mouth as often as I used to.

Josh settles in a chair. "I can watch again now if you like," he tells Darryl. "It won't be much longer."

"Oh, uh, thanks." Darryl turns so she can look at the interior of the fairground again. But after a moment, she says in a low voice. "Is, uh, everyone gonna...going to...think what Trudi thought?"

Josh shrugs, flushing slightly. "Likely. I guess we didn't think about that. West should've set her straight but I guess he don't want to let on what he's doing for us—soon as he does, she's dragged in too."

Darryl's silent for a moment. "Well, too late now. We've got to be here. For Dad."

27

"Saint Des knows the truth, anyway," says Josh, as though that settles that.

Silence falls as we watch a vehicle driving slowly past while several teen boys chuck bales of straw from the back ready to spread over the marked pathways, which are still mostly snow at the moment but will be mud soon enough, unless the temperature drops a lot.

Lights are coming on along the pathways as twilight settles in. Suddenly, three flares streak up from the center of the fairground, making me jump as they open into green starbursts. A cacophony of horns and claxons and cheers splits the comparative quiet as every vehicle in the ring honks and flashes every horn or light they've got.

Josh raises the windows, then activates the strobe on top of the turret, leans on the turret horn control and whoops loudly. After a moment of wide-eyed shock at the noise, Darryl and I join in. Guess this is why Josh insisted on shutting Kiko into the partially sound-proofed critter cage as soon as we arrived.

When the racket dies down, Josh lowers the windows again and grins. "Ring's complete," he tells us. "Dusk has fallen. Happy Saint Des's Day! It's fair time. Grab your hoods and claw necklaces!"

Already, doors are opening all along the inside of the ring and people are getting down from the vehicles. I'm used to thinking of a HabVi holding about three to four guys, five at most, but whole families are pouring out. The 'Vi next to us has disgorged eight children so far, and counting. Guess if the 'Vi has even three guys, and they've each got kids... They must've left most of their equipment behind to make enough sleeping berths.

"It'll just be food and story-telling tonight," Josh is saying, when I join him and Darryl below. "The action is all tomorrow."

"Sounds good to me," says Darryl, putting on her parka.

Josh has just zipped up his coat and fitted some odd contraptions to his forearms. Long, thin rectangles, with two straps to hold them on and some sort of control on the inside of his wrist.

"What are those?" I ask.

"What, *these*?" Josh flings his arms out, flicking his wrists, and Darryl and I both recoil as brightly colored arcs burst out over his arms, almost like wings, with an impressively loud *clack-clack-screech*. "You mean my frights?"

"Your what?" asks Darryl, stepping closer to examine one.

I do the same. The things seem to be made of shimmery multi-colored mirror-like material. They unfold from each forearm like a fan, flipping up to rest against his upper arm, making an impressive arc of color and reflected light.

"Frights," grins Josh, who's clearly saved these for a

surprise. "Traditional diversion device from the early days after the Rewilding. When HabVis weren't as good and couldn't go so many places and hunters did a lot more foot patrolling, and they were scrambling for anything and everything that might give them an edge. Something comes at you, you flip your frights at them and try to scare it off, make yourself look bigger. Like a dilophosaur does with its frill. Can sometimes work with velociraptors or deinons, or even a solitary Dakotaraptor if you're *very* lucky and it ain't too hungry. Mostly worn at fairs these days, but occasionally useful. Some hunters totally dismiss 'em, especially city-borns, but I'd still wear 'em if I was going on a long jaunt, sure as sure."

He reaches to each arm, carefully refolding each 'fright,' his expression grave. "See, this is my Uncle Z's pair, 'cause my dad...he *was* wearing his when he... Y'know, since he was going a way out-Vi. But no use against a nesting she-rex, unfortunately."

"They're *cool*," I say. "Can I get some?"

"They're usually given as gifts on a special occasion—or inherited. Be seen as kinda presumptuous to buy them for yourself."

"Oh." Hunters. So many traditions. Even after almost a year there's so much to learn. I pick up the beautifully decorated hood Josh gave me and carefully pull it over my head, tugging the warm fur capelet down over my shoulders. Hoods are certainly the thing for a midwinter fair since they go *over* your proper parka! "Uh...thanks again for this, Josh." It's his uncle's, it must mean a lot to him.

He shrugs. "I couldn't keep it forever."

Why not? is my farmer-born thought, but he's a full-time 'Vi-dweller, so he's probably right. My stomach rumbles. "I'm famished."

"Then let's go find something good to eat," says Josh. "No fasting on Saint Des's Day!"

Yeah, it's a solemnity for anyone who lives out-city!

JOSHUA

I polish off my last bite of hog roast and lick my fingers clean. After that dawn-to-dusk, three-day drive to get here on time, I'm hungry. At least Darryl and Harry are both now experienced enough to spell me at the wheel over easier terrain.

Darryl's just passed the last of her roll to Harry, who's doing a good impression of a hungry hatchling, so I look around for dessert. Soon enough we're tucking into a big bag of donuts.

"I know you said about sticking together," says Darryl softly, after she's consumed two of the soft, sugary treats, "but we've more chances of hearing something about Dad if we split up."

"Not tonight," I say firmly. "We'll see tomorrow, when it's daylight. I guess you're both old enough to know this, but—no way, no how do I know everyone here and not all people are good, right?"

Darryl makes a face, but nods. Dad and Uncle Z woulda never let me roam the fairground alone in the dark, even when I were Harry's age. With a group of other fourteen year olds, sure. But he ain't part of one. And Darryl, who's pretty for a hunter thank-you-very-much-Trudi, never mind for a farmgirl? Just no.

A dark hand dips into the donut bag, making me spin around. "Hey!"

But it's just West, biting into his stolen dessert with relish. I relax. "Oh, there you guys are."

The other two are behind him. I hold out the bag as they reach for it.

"Thought you weren't coming," says Thiago, fishing out what proves to be the last donut and eyeing it with anticipation.

"Yeah, well, we figured we're running out of chances to find out what we need to find out."

"That's certainly true," says West, swallowing his last bite of donut and eyeing the empty bag.

"We're gonna need more," I say. "Ed didn't even get one."

"I'm on it," says Ed, and heads for the stall, pausing to flick his frights at a large group of children, who giggle and cheer.

Smoke drifts from the bonfires as people begin to gather for the storytelling. Children dash past, screeching and laughing. Excitement surges, riding the growing darkness like a tide as frights flick and clack and screech on all sides. Harry swells happily as West congratulates him on the new Utahraptor claw on his necklace, while Darryl looks on with an unconsciously proud smile.

Despite my worries about whether we'll actually find out anything about William Franklyn and what we'll do if we don't—or if we do, come to that—it sure is good to be at a fair again!

HARRY

Ed has *awesome* frights, sticking up over his shoulders like twin swords and folding out down the length of his back! And I thought *Josh's* were cool. I've already seen an old guy—an 'Elder' who Josh nodded to and called 'sir'—with a set that arch right up high behind his head, and a younger man with a pair of 'fixed frights' that go from arms to legs like bat wings.

And the outfits! Our heavily decorated hoods and even Josh's chaps are *plain*! Some older guys have full knee-length fur coats with feathers sticking out all the way around, just like on their chaps, to say nothing of all the bone beads, teeth, claws, feather quill-work, tassels, and intricately engraved or enameled metal pieces all over them. Some guys don't wear hoods, but sort of cage-like hats of massive utahraptor claws, lined with fur. Hoods are more common, designs varying from plainer fur to various feathered styles. My favorite is one with feathery ear tufts—like on an eagle owl.

Josh's chaps are Utah-raptor grey, but West's are stark white, off-setting his skin-color magnificently. Thiago is all in black, matching his dark hair, every feather purple or green, very smart, and I did a double-take when I first saw Ed, because his chaps are buttercup yellow—also matching his hair. More or less. Eye-watering. Cheerful, though.

Boy, is it a riot of color!

West isn't wearing any frights, maybe because he's sporting an enormous wolf fur cloak instead of a parka, fastened with a button at the shoulder, with a massive fall of fur hanging down his back. Darryl strokes the soft fur admiringly, making Thiago and Ed crack up for some unknown reason and West smile tolerantly.

After some more donut demolition Josh also tugs on the long tail, teasingly. "I'm guessing Trudi's off-shift before the storytelling starts, huh, if the courting cloak is out?"

"Sure is." West checks the time, refusing to be drawn. "I'm off to get her, in fact."

"And...that's it," says Ed, watching him walk away. "We're gonna be ignored for the rest of the evening, now."

"For the rest of our *lives*," Thiago advises him. "Get used to it."

"Nah, I've a better idea. If you can't beat 'em, join 'em. Yeah, you know who I mean. She still ain't married yet."

"Don't mean it's you she's waiting for."

"When I've got a fence to offer her, I'm gonna find out."

DARRYL

By the time West rejoins us, we've moved to one of the bonfires ready for the storytelling, settling on the log seats that are scattered all around the fire. West's cloak suddenly makes sense, because it's now fastened with another button at the very end of that long tail, keeping it snug around both him *and* Trudi.

I try to get a look at what she's wearing under it. She notices, and holds the cloak aside to show me her full-length dress. Long sleeved, high necked, trimmed with fur, and she's got on soft moccasins, disappearing up her legs, but she's considerably more elegant than most women, who're buttoned up in their parkas and well-booted.

"Perks of courting," she tells me, with a wink. "You get to dress up and still be warm."

Her hair's been braided with a ton of feathers now, fanning out from under a small fur cap and shimmering iridescent in the firelight. It looks *amazing*. "You look great," I tell her, hoping that's an acceptable hunter compliment.

"Thanks. That's a nice hood." She sounds sincere, though I bet she can tell it's a boy's one, or was until recently.

She snuggles with West under the cloak and they get wrapped up in each other in a way that reminds me painfully of Dad and Carol. I go to sit with Harry and Josh near Thiago and Ed, still peeking at women's outfits. More of them seem to be dressed in practical modern parkas, although with fancy hoods, maybe because so many of them are wrangling small children. One little boy is ripping handfuls of feathers from his distracted father's leg-wear. Oh dear.

Some women do wear chaps despite the knee-high menace—the huntresses?—others wear divided skirts, often feathered in a similar way—campmakers? Or is it just personal choice? The ones in full traditional formal wear have coats that flare at the hips, often with heavy decoration across the shoulders and upper back, almost mane-like. They mostly have a lot more embroidery than the guys and far fewer teeth and claws. I'd say female hunter fashion leans more towards elegance, male more towards display. Like with birds and raptors, I guess!

I've seen photos of hunter gear, of course, but I didn't realize they wear it so much when they get together—and, honestly, the photos don't do it justice. Did photos of this sort of thing consciously or

36

subconsciously inspire Carol's final set of designs?

Thiago comes back from the stalls with bags full of chestnuts and marshmallows so we start making good use of the bonfire. West and Trudi are soon feeding each other sweet treats with their forks. Harry alternates between staring and trying not to look. I know how he feels.

Fortunately, with a great puff of smoke and sparks from the bonfire, the first story-teller leaps into sight. He's wearing multiple frights, bigger and more dramatic than any we've seen, and he flicks them all at once—*clack-screeeeeeeech!*—causing silence to fall.

I expect him to start a story, but instead he launches straight into the centerpiece prayer for the chaplet of Saint Desmond, only he doesn't just pray it, he *prays* it. Someone beats a drum and someone else plays a haunting flute, sending shivers down my spine as the prayer unfolds.

O Lord, you know of what we are made,
dust and clay.
Our days are like grass,
we bloom like a flower in the meadow;
the wind blows and we are gone.
If you take our breath, we return to earth,
and our plans this day come to nothing.

The haircut I gave Josh on the way here pops back into my mind. Or rather, him gathering up the loose hair afterwards and putting it carefully into that decorated bag of his. *Just in case.*

I don't ever want to be burying that bag, wrapped in one of his shirts, in place of him. *Or* burying him, either.

Okay, so Harry and I both made our own bags months ago, under Josh's direction, and I cut off a few inches of hair to put in mine and Harry's been saving his trimmings. It *is* a good idea. It's just all a little more *memento mori* than we were used to on the farm.

Hunters are big on *memento mori*. Most people skip this centerpiece prayer, but not hunters...

You know my resting and my rising,
marking when I work or lie down,
all my ways are naked before you.
If I assume feathers at dawn
and soar to the heavens, you are there.
If I lie in the grave, you are there.
Your right hand grips me forever.

The storyteller finishes on his knees, arms outstretched to the night sky, and holds a long silence, like a baited breath before a storm...

Until, finally, "Saint Desmond the Hermit, we invoke your powerful intercession for the peace of this fair and the safety of all here."

With that, he launches into the familiar chaplet. Everyone joins in, and for some minutes the night echoes with "Jesus, I trust in you," until with one last rousing chorus of...

From T. rex' jaws
From raptor's claws,
From life indoors,
From all our flaws,
Deliver us, Lord.
And smile upon us,
Mother mild.

...the chaplet is complete.

The drums and the flute start again, and the storyteller begins to narrate the story of the Rewilding, of how most folk fled to the cities, but how the hunter-born's ancestors stayed. Trappers, native Americans, ranchers, smallholders, country-townsfolk... Anyone who didn't want to live in a cage.

I've never heard the history from quite this perspective before and it's spell-binding. At dramatic moments during the tale he tosses powders onto the bonfire to make it spark and flare and the audience flick their frights with him at the right times, making the night echo.

Far more men than women have frights, so I guess

they're connected to actually hunting. I can guess what Harry's thinking and I kinda agree: I wish someone would gift me a pair. I'd love to be able to join in!

HARRY

The bonfires are getting rowdier, now. The storytellers have finished and most of the children and families have disappeared. West sets off to walk Trudi back to her uncle's 'Vi—he's an Elder, apparently, him *and* another uncle *and* an aunt—so West don't dare put a foot wrong. Ed is hanging out, real casual, like, with a group that includes the woman he was talking about earlier, with Thiago in support.

Josh says it's time to head back to the 'Vi and Darryl seems to be of the same mind, so off we go.

"Is there going to be Mass?" Darryl asks Josh hopefully.

He shakes his head. "Nah, not this year."

Darryl looks disappointed, and after that extra-ordinary Ash Wednesday we had, I feel kinda disappointed too. Father Ben heard our confessions and gave us Communion both times we saw him, but it's been ages since we got to Mass. It's not actually a sin if you're a long way from church, apparently, but it feels weird. We keep having Adoration, though.

Father Ben is keen to bring Josh's 'sacramental life' up-to-date but there's been no question of him spending enough time with us to do it, yet. "Well, you're baptized, at least," he sighed, "that's the most important thing, in your profession." Leading Josh to give him a lecture on how most hunters die in their beds of old age, thank you very much, which was pretty funny.

"We'll definitely have a proper hymn-singing at midsummer, with drums and flutes, and sometimes there is Mass," Josh adds, "but it's so hard to get a priest out here for a fair. The last one the bishop sent was a nightmare. Went back to the city and tried to file all kinds of complaints about who knows what. There's a pair of hunter-borns in seminary at the moment—twins—and they're supposed to be assigned to 'the hunting community' once they're...er...priested. If that bishop sticks to what he said."

"What did the priest complain about?" I ask.

"Oh, er, he said kids were carrying weapons, which is nonsense because little kids can't carry rifles at the fair. Only once they're old enough not to put 'em down and leave 'em and above all, to keep their temper when the kid from that other camp drops a mouse down their neck."

It's true, I haven't seen a kid younger than about twelve with a rifle, though most adults have one over their shoulder. Since all hunter kids will own their own by age seven, even if they're not allowed free access to it—like most farm kids—I guess this rule counts as responsible restraint—at least by hunter standards. I haven't worked this long for Josh without catching on that self-control is the number one virtue as far as hunters are concerned—and it's obviously drilled into their children from a very young age.

"What else?"

"Oh, he got real upset about *car seats*. Or lack of. Seemed to think every kid should travel in an *actual* seat, can you believe." Josh pauses to touch the door control on the 'Vi, then waves along the ring to where a father is tossing sleepy or giggling kids up into the side doorway of a HabVi, where they're caught by another father and deposited inside. "I mean, how the heck does he think you're gonna get them all here?"

"How *do* they secure them?" asks Darryl curiously.

"Bungee 'em to the walls, mostly, and go slow and careful. It's largely off-road, no city-idiots to collide with."

"You should get Father Ben to come," I tell him. "He wouldn't be silly about things like that."

"Huh, that's a real good idea. I should mention his name to Trudi. Her uncle and aunt are two of the main organizers."

DARRYL

By the time my watch is over in the morning and we've all gobbled some breakfast the fair is in full swing, though it's mostly children and family groups heading out of their 'Vis. I guess a lot of the single guys who were getting raucous around the bonfires when we called it a night are sleeping in, especially if they had night watches.

Apparently if you get caught skipping a watch—or drunk on watch—your whole 'Vi has to stay at the end of the fair and fill in the latrines, which cuts down offenses. But there's a ton of redundancy built into the schedule in case people do it anyway. And a bunch of experienced hunters carried out a foot patrol of the fairground at dawn, as well—just to check.

"It's mostly the children's racing this morning," says Josh as we put our boots on. "But that's fun to watch. Bring Kiko, it'll be quieter this morning, and there's a pet competition."

Harry hits the door 'open' button and moves to jump out but Josh grabs him. "Hey, didn't you hear the horn just then?"

"What?" Harry looks blank—then starts back as about ten or twenty ornithomimus thunder past outside, running hard, each with a child on its back.

"Just inside the ring doubles up as the race track. Largest circumference available," says Josh. "Get out of the way when the horn goes."

"Right."

We scoot across the danger zone and head into the interior of the fairground. Frozen mud crunches under our feet, our breath misting in the air. Soon we reach the collecting paddock beside the start line, which teams with over-excited children and ornis.

The tall, leggy 'saurs, which city-folk often describe as being like ostriches with tails, wear fairly plain leather saddles, for the most part, like at a country rodeo, but their racing bridles drip with bone beads and teeth and feather embroidery. Large blinkers screen the ornis' eyes from distraction, though most in the paddock are still wearing their blindfolds to keep them calmer in the chaos.

Despite the super-elaborate bridles, it's a familiar sight from my own childhood, and I can't help smiling as Kiko stares doubtfully at all the activity. "Huh, this brings it back."

Harry gazes wistfully at the scene. At eleven, he was still just small enough to ride our orni—well, his orni, by then—at the local rodeo. It's been much longer for me.

Josh leans his hands on the rail, smiling too as he watches the bustle—or, especially, the ornis, which range from very fine to old and scruffy.

"Did you ever race, Josh?" I ask, stroking Kiko to keep him calm. I bet Josh was good at it.

To my surprise, he replies, "Only once. It were just a wild one, though the best we could catch, no fancy bloodlines, so I were thrilled to come fourth. It went for a good price, with that rosette fluttering on its bridle."

At our surprised looks, he explains, "We had to sell

her, right after the race. Needed the pen back."

Of course. It's easy to see Josh's childhood as utterly free and unconstrained but living entirely in a HabVi has just as many constraints as being raised in one place on a farm—they're just different ones. No space to keep full formal gear—*or* large pets. Even now, I keep forgetting that.

Josh raises a hand suddenly, waving at a child. "Hey, kid, bring your orni here."

The boy approaches, leading a large russet colored female. Not a young animal, but still in her prime.

"You're from the Fischer camp, right?" says Josh.

"Yeah, I'm Tahatan. You're the raptor whisperer."

"Trot her up, will you. I think there's something wrong with her leg."

Horror spreads over Tahatan's face. From his age and size, this is probably his last year orni-riding. "She was fine earlier!" But he's already leading the orni at a jog.

Josh watches, then ducks under the rail and goes to lift the closest leg, feeling his way down it.

"Here," he says, stopping on her lower bone. "She's throwing out a massive splint. She can't run today."

"No! She's *gotta* be okay! This is my last year!"

"Feel her leg, Tahatan."

Reluctantly, Tahatan lets Josh show him what he's found, his face scrunching up dismay.

"She was out training just before we set off and she

45

was *fine*," he says quickly. "I'm sure she'll be okay."

"Training around a little camp fence ain't racing flat-out on a full track. How long have you had her?"

Tahatan looks nervous. "Six years."

"Fond of her?"

"Yeah..."

"Well, I'm telling you, she runs today, she'll likely break her leg halfway round. And then your dad will bring you your rifle and tell you that you know what you have to do. So race her or not, she's your orni. But know that's how it will probably end."

The kid's lip trembles, his face screwing up tighter and tighter. He's trying not to cry. But, finally, he nods jerkily at Josh.

"Thanks, Mr. Wilson," he squeaks. And he leads his orni from the paddock. A man and a woman approach him and he starts arguing with them. Looks like his parents are set on him racing. But eventually he leads the orni away toward the ring—he's going to put it back in his 'Vi's rear pen.

"Good boy," murmurs Josh.

"That's sad." I can't help feeling for the kid's bitter disappointment.

"Yeah," agrees Josh. "Real test of character, though. In their last year, some kids would run the poor creature and hope for the best."

"Serve them right if they broke their own neck when it went down," says Harry, who I'm still not sure has got over selling that beloved orni of ours a few years back.

"Yep," drawls Josh.

"Josh!" A teenager a few years younger than me appears, towing a very small girl who in turn tows an orni, all saddled ready to race and towering over her. "Can you check Susie's orni?"

"Sure." Josh inspects the 'saur and watches him jog around, then grins. "He's on top form."

"Great!" The teenager hefts her little sister up into the saddle. "Now, *don't* fall off or mum will *kill you!*"

"I won't!" the tiny girl squeals, turning the orni towards the start line as someone with a megaphone starts calling for "Junior fives."

The teenager glances at me, then grins at Josh. "So, is that your farmgirl? Well, *I* think it's *romantic.*"

"It ain't like th—" Josh starts, but the girl's run off after her sister, shouting, "Wait, silly!" as she tries to remove the forgotten blindfold.

Josh sighs and shakes his head. I guess it's not my imagination that a lot of people have been looking at us. He's already repeated that it "ain't like that" to a couple of stern-faced Elders—and so far they all seem to have accepted his word. But everyone else must figure that if the organizers let us in, we can't be kidnapped—so they're falling back on the other explanation.

Great. Just great.

HARRY

Josh is kept busy inspecting a steady stream of mounts at the request of cautious riders or relatives who know or know of him, though he breaks off for a minute to point Darryl to the pet show. I hover beside him, patting ornis and occasionally helping adjust a harness buckle. It gives me a painful feeling in my stomach, seeing all this. Three years ago, I could still ride.

During a lull in his role as orni whisperer Josh asks if I miss it. He must see the way I'm looking around.

"Yeah. I sold my orni two years ago, when I realized I really *wasn't* going to be able to ride her again. She looked so bored, y'know? It's stupid, but I just don't think I really grasped it immediately, even when I'd had to stop getting on her 'cos I was too big."

Josh just nods. "The little death."

"Huh?"

"Hunters call it 'the little death.' When a kid gets too big to ride an orni anymore. It's like, the first big step out of childhood. Childhood takes time to die."

The little death. Yeah. "That's a good name."

The paddock slowly clears as the various categories run their races. There won't be any adult racing. Few adults ride. Going around and around the inside of the home fence is dull as ditchwater and riding outside the fence is like delivering take-out to carni'saurs. The few that can't quit riding tend to go work on a racing ranch with thoroughbred dracorex, which are the adult-sized

48

equivalent of an orni, or one of the few remaining horse ranches if they're old-fashioned.

Technicolor arrive as the last race is starting. "You wanna get some lunch?" asks West.

"Yep," says Josh. "Something hot."

Definitely something hot. It's been fun, but I'm getting chilled. The day hasn't warmed up much. Oh! Darryl's back, standing with her elbows on the rail. Kiko sits on her shoulder, a large rosette fluttering from his leash. Guess he impressed the judges! But after everyone congratulates her she takes him back to the 'Vi while we go to join a line for food. The fair's only going to get noisier from now on. People are starting to flick their frights again and Kiko doesn't like it.

We retreat with something hot and tasty to a quiet table to eat. Well, two tables, though close together, to make it look very casual. We could go into one of the 'Vis for privacy—and warmth—but if someone takes pictures that's evidence of conspiracy with us against Technicolor.

We haven't seen them since New Year and Trudi's on shift again and not here so I immediately ask, "Have you heard anything about Dad?"

My heart sinks as they shake their heads. Darryl was right that we needed to come here. We're getting nowhere.

"Have you two thought of anything that it could be other than straight kidnapping?" asks West—as usual.

49

"'Cause I'm sorry, kidnapping carries a minimum of twenty years in prison. I can't believe anyone would think that what they could get from your father would be worth that risk. Now, a rich farmer like that neighbor of yours, Maurice Carr, maybe. But they took your dad. It don't make sense."

West's conviction that it *don't make sense* hasn't wavered, but Darryl and I still can't think of any other reason for Dad to be taken or killed.

When we shake our heads, West hesitates. "Then...it's been almost a year. I don't know how much longer there's any point you doing this to yourselves."

"It's not a year *yet*," I say fiercely. "What if they're waiting for Darryl to be eighteen?"

West shakes his head, looking at Josh, not me. "Mebbe you *should* think about leaving Exception, Josh. The city-folk are still looking for you. That frilly city-lady came to the 'Vi-park again the last time we were there and gave us the third degree. Again. They've obviously got their eye on us. We made sure one of us was with the vehicle all the time, and we searched it as soon as we left, to make sure they hadn't managed to slip a tracker on board. But they're not letting it alone, Josh. You need to start thinking about yourself, instead of a dead man."

Josh shoots Darryl and me a look. "We don't know he's dead, West!"

"You've no evidence he's alive, neither. No one's

gonna keep someone this long, just for ransom."

"The priest hasn't found nothing out?" asks Thiago tensely.

Darryl shakes her head. "No. Last time we saw him, all he had to say was that Uncle Mau was fretting because Fernanda 'Frilly' Matthews had been around to interview him yet again and he was worried he might've let on how long we've known Father Ben and how much we rely on him. So we're not gonna meet Father Ben any more often than absolutely necessary."

West shakes his head. "The net's closing around you. What if they manage to find some way to take us out of the picture, even temporarily? We're keeping our noses squeaky-clean, but they might play dirty. You have to have fuel and ammo, so what will you do then?"

"I do have other friends," says Josh.

"Not like us and this is getting too serious to trust to any old acquaintance, not when anyone who helps you can be had up. I'm just saying, Josh. You *need* to be thinking about leaving or you're gonna to end up in prison."

"*I—*"

West cuts off Josh's fierce words. "Or free and eaten, yeah, okay. 'Cause that's so much better."

I shift nervously, watching Josh. Darryl watches him too. Ed doesn't say anything—right now he's busy petting someone's dog—but considering what he was saying last night... And West and Thiago are *definitely* getting more and more unhappy about the whole situation. How long before Josh starts listening to them? Heck, even I keep thinking about leaving Exception and not being hunted anymore, and it's my dad. If Josh wanted to go, who could blame him?

Trying to save Dad has to be the right thing to do, surely? Or...is there a point at which it becomes... selfish? The uncomfortable thought wriggles through my tummy like a worm.

Josh glances at us again. "Look, let's enjoy the fair and keep our ears peeled. Mebbe we'll hear something."

Thiago snorts. He stuffs the last of his burger in his mouth, chews and swallows, then straightens. "Well, I'm off to the rodeo, see if I can break my fool neck before my momma has to hear that I'm doing time for child kidnapping."

"*Thiago!*" West shoots him a look. "Cool it; we did this sort of thing all the time for Isaiah."

"Josh *belonged* with Isaiah!" snaps Thiago. "It were plain wrong, them trying to take him away." He jabs a finger at me and Darryl. "Them two don't belong with Josh. It ain't the same, and *we're* gonna pay for it!" He stamps off.

Josh winces. "How is his momma?"

"Not good. Very, very frail. She ain't gonna be around much longer and worrying about this is making it worse for him. He knows what it would mean to her if he could bring her to live at his very own camp before the end. That woman's been bottom dog in one camp or another her whole life."

Josh looks uncomfortable. "Can't you just pop the question to Trudi and get your camp set up?"

West makes a face. "I feel real uncomfortable offering myself as her provider and protector with this hanging over us. Real dishonest. I've gone slow enough to show I'm serious and I respect her, but at our age... She wants kids, Josh. She ain't gonna wait around for me forever. I don't know what to do."

Josh winces. "I really am sorry to be asking this of you guys. I mean, I guess Thiago *is* right. Darryl and Harry don't *strictly*—"

West cuts him off. "You may not have a piece of paper to say you're family, but you look like one to me."

Josh glances at Darryl. "You *do* know we *ain't*—"

"I know you *ain't*; I don't mean it that way. Don't worry about Thiago, Josh. He's a worrier, always has been, you know that. You *need* to get yourself out of this situation—for your sake, just as much as ours—but until then, we've still got your back."

Josh shoots West and Ed a grateful look. "Thanks, West. You guys are the best."

West shrugs; Ed shrugs. Yeah, hunters are a real demonstrative lot. Make farmers look emotional!

"Guess we'd better go watch him fall off," says

53

West.

"Someone needs to be ready to laugh," says Ed.

"Yeah, what are friends for?" says Josh, winking at me and making me laugh too.

DARRYL

The arenas are set back slightly from the main area. The one we're approaching is crowded, but not so much that we can't find a place beside the rail. Very high rails, easily fourteen-foot, though with gaps large enough for a man to slide through. We look between the most eye-level gap, but there's nothing to see at the moment.

"Watch yourself if it comes this way," cautions Josh. "Not all the claws are capped."

West chuckles. "Oh boy, Joshua Wilson is suddenly the responsible adult. If Zech and Isaiah could see this. To think we used to have to all watch non-stop that you didn't sneak behind the scenes to try to make friends with them rodeo steeds."

"*So* weird," adds Ed. "Our little Joshy-woshy, all grown up."

I try not to laugh as Josh puts on a dignified expression and ignores them. Harry snorts.

The chute gate on the far side of the arena flies back and in a blur of feathers the rodeo animal is out of the pen, springing immensely high and spinning lightning-fast as it tries to throw off the hunter on its back.

"*Holy—*" Harry breaks off in time, but I know how he feels.

It's an honest-to-God *Dakotaraptor*!

HARRY

The raptor moves so fast I can hardly take anything in. It's not long before the guy on its back comes flying off, rolling as he hits the dust. The raptor charges at him, screeching, but he takes a header at the fence and makes it through the gap. Only as the raptor slows and stalks around the arena, hissing, do I see that it's muzzled and has its killing claws capped. The wing-arm claws are bare, though.

A strange saddle is strapped to its back, with two long poles sticking out diagonally towards the ground—oh, to stop it getting down and rolling. At almost a third of a ton, you don't want a Dakotaraptor landing on you and they're smart and agile enough to try it immediately.

Darryl whistles. "Raptor rodeo? So that isn't just a tall tale."

"Sure ain't," grins Josh. "Beats your country rodeo hands down."

"Yeah, I mean, you still use *bulls*," says Ed, his blue eyes twinkling.

"*Boring*," adds West.

I'd love to defend country ways, but after seeing

this...how can I!

"So, uh, Thiago's gonna do this?" I ask.

"Sure," says West. "If it weren't for you guys, I'd have a go myself."

"Uh, we ain't stopping you." Are we?

"Thiago's already in line. We can't all risk getting injured, not right now."

"Oh." Guess we are, at that.

"Do you ever do this?" Darryl asks Josh.

"Sure." He grins. "Though there's less and less of these games anyone will let me compete in."

"Why."

He shrugs, flushing.

West replies instead. "It makes it too boring for everyone if they know who's gonna win."

"And the moment Josh gets near a raptor—everyone knows who's gonna win," drawls Ed.

"Even the rodeo," says West. "He had the dang thing standing still in the end, one year. That was when the organizers decided he could still get on one if he wanted but not be placed."

"Good job he ain't competitive," says Ed. "Thiago would've lost it with them. It ain't really fair."

Josh just shrugs. "I don't care. I don't wanna spoil it for everyone."

"I thought domesticating raptors was illegal?" says Darryl, watching as the Dakotaraptor allows itself to be herded out of the arena by two handlers with electric stock prods, seeming pretty unconcerned by the whole business.

"They don't keep 'em. Zoo-tame 'em just before the fair, get 'em used to wearing the saddle, nothing more, take 'em straight to zoos after. They can't really be called domesticated. They'll only have a handful, anyway. Just enough to let 'em have a break between rides and not get too used to it."

"And seriously, who's gonna tell?" murmurs Ed. "Or believe it..."

True, even most farmers take it for a tall tale.

"Do you use any other animals for rodeo?" I ask.

"Mostly just raptors, nowadays," says Josh. "Rex rodeo used to be the big thing, back in the day. But now everything to do with rex is so restricted, and DAPdep monitor 'em all so closely."

"Yeah, can't just 'borrow' one and hope they won't notice." Ed sounds regretful.

"Rex? How does that work? You put a saddle like that on?" I try to picture it, a saddled rex... Darryl screws up her face as though picturing it too.

"Nah, no saddles for rex," says Ed.

"Don't need 'em," says Josh. "They don't drop and roll, like raptors. They can't jump up as fast, so getting down on the ground makes 'em feel vulnerable. If you get one the right size—juvenile is good—you can sit on its shoulders and hook your feet in under the armpits, and that's how you try to stay on."

"Half the skill was in getting your heels hooked in," says West, nodding. "If you could hook in, you had a good chance of staying on. At least for a while."

"Muzzled, of course." The other two laugh as though Josh has said something obvious. "It was still real dangerous, though. People sometimes got stepped on after they came off. And that's bad enough with a Dakotaraptor."

Darryl winces—I wince too. Even a juvenile rex weighs about four or five tons.

"Hence the expression, *it was a right rex rodeo*," adds Josh. "Meaning, incredibly dangerous."

We look around eagerly as a fresh Dakotaraptor bursts from the chute, another guy clinging to its back for a brief, whirlwind ride.

He comes off quick, leaps up and dives for the fence. Hooks up his belt buckle, though, and can't get through, yelping as the raptor slashes the seat of his pants open with a wing claw. The crowd roars with laughter. But he gets free—and through—before the raptor can get him again.

"Heck, this is crazy enough," mutters Darryl.

"Mostly minor injuries, though," says Josh. "Not like Pachy ballet."

I'm about to ask what Pachy ballet is when I notice the next guy being loaded into the chute. "Oh, look, it's Thiago!"

Thiago stays on much longer than either of the

other guys but bounces off a harness pole and lands badly, lying there clearly too winded to rise. He's gonna get clawed! But the raptor's triumphant approach checks as Josh screeches something convincingly raptor-ish at the top of his lungs. It spins around and dashes towards our end of the arena, fierce eyes looking for the strange raptor.

Thiago's getting up, finally, so Josh keeps the raptor engaged in conversation until he's staggered to the side and made it out of the pen. When he joins us he has to endure some good-natured ribbing from his 'Vi-mates—but he mutters a thank you to Josh and it sounds like he got a good time so he seems much happier, despite having a bunch of broken feathers on his chaps. "Plenty more where those came from," he says.

I go back to watching the other contestants. Boy, do those raptors leap high! No wonder people want to get on them.

"Is there, like, a junior class?" I ask, without thinking.

Oh great. I get laughed at.

"No," says West, eventually getting his breath back. "There ain't a junior class for this."

"Funny, that," says Ed.

"Actually, they gave me a watch shift, right?" I've gotta go do that soon, in fact. "So if I count as a man for *that*..."

"No," says Darryl.

"No," says Josh.

Their tone... I don't even bother to argue. So that's that.

Spoilsports.

DARRYL

No doubt remembering the penalty for missing a watch, Harry hurries off back to the 'Vi in good time. We agree to wait here until he returns, to keep things simple. I sure don't mind watching the rodeo for an hour. Heck, is it fast and furious. And addictive. It makes normal rodeo look slow and tame.

West, Thiago, and Ed head off after a while to get a drink—or possibly some ice for Thiago's bruises—but Josh and I keep watching. I'm starting to get a better feel for the skill of the competitors as Josh points things out.

The trick seems to be to make sure you're thrown as the raptor's coming down, but as horizontally as possible. One guy totally miss-times it and soars right over the fence, landing with a crack of breaking bone. He's carried away on a stretcher, cursing and begging for a drink. At least he's conscious.

I only see one woman compete. She stays on a long time, though. I wonder if I could do this? I mean, maybe in a year or two. Once we've found Dad. It would be crazy to do it today.

Josh shows no sign of getting in the line—guess he also doesn't want to risk getting hurt right now—though he does sigh wistfully a few times as we watch particularly spectacular rides.

Harry's back before we know it, eager to see more rodeo. It takes a while, but eventually I remember that we're not just here to watch people fall off raptors, super-entertaining as it may be. *Dad...*

"Hey, Josh? Since Harry's back, should we, uh, walk around and chat to people or something?"

He looks startled, then slightly sheepish, and so does Harry. Guess they got caught up in the rodeo too.

"Yeah, let's head for the competition tents. Looking at all the entries is a great way to strike up conversations with a lotta people."

We head that way, but we haven't gone far when...

"So, what do we have here?" The loud, cutting voice brings Josh to a halt, his shoulders tensing. "Looks like Joshua Wilson is just as big a hypocrite as his father ever was. What a surprise."

HARRY

I spin around, looking for the owner of the sneering voice. Seven guys are spread across the path behind us and a number of them look close-related, the same dark hair and white-Chinese-Native American mix features. I'm not sure who spoke.

61

Josh turns around more slowly. Everyone nearby is watching and listening with keen attention.

"My dad weren't a hypocrite, Jason," Josh speaks clearly and audibly, "and I ain't one neither. I ain't done nothing wrong, and Saint Des is my witness."

The guy in the middle, slightly older than West, tall, moderate-build, with weather-beaten skin and a slightly weasely face—Jason, presumably—snorts. "Not what the city-folk say."

"Since when do hunters care what the city-folk say?"

"Since they're pestering everyone in the 'Vi-park every time they go in-city, mebbe?"

"It don't take long to say you don't know nothing."

"You're a stinking hypocrite, Wilson, just like your father."

Josh remains very tense. Darryl stands stiffly beside him, her fingers clenched on the strap of her rifle where it runs across her chest. We're badly outnumbered.

"Seriously, Jason?" Josh's voice is sharp. "You really wanna discuss *why* Dad called you out that day, right here at the fair, where your wife might hear?"

Jason's eyes narrow and his fists clench. "You tell lies about me and you'll get what's coming to you." He shifts forward slightly.

"Peace of the fair!" shouts an onlooker in a cautioning tone.

"I ain't telling lies about no one," says Josh, and

62

makes to turn away.

"You'd better not," mocks Jason. "'Cause Zechariah ain't here to protect you anymore, is he? And Isaiah's long since *digested*. You've got no one at your back but a farmboy and your little—" He uses a word I don't recognize but I know he's talking about Darryl.

Josh goes rigid, spinning around again.

"Go wash your mouth out, Jason! We don't want nothing to do with you!"

He catches Darryl by the elbow, and me too, trying to hurry us away, but Jason follows.

"Oh, you *don't*, huh?" Jason sneers, then eyes Darryl again. Clearly even this spino spawn has the self-control not to actually attack Josh—but he'd love Josh to fly at *him*, wouldn't he? "So, not like *that*, is that how you'd have it? Joshua Wilson is just looking after the poor little orphans, is *that* how it is? Out of the goodness of his lovely shining heart? Not wanting a *thing* in return?"

"We're not all as sick as you, Jason," Josh snaps, still towing us away. I want to turn back and punch Jason myself, though he's Dad's age.

Self-control, Harry. Be a man. Don't let Josh down...

"Look at all the poor little orphans, sticking together. Such a *shame* when fathers get *eaten*, isn't it? Do they miss him *terribly*?"

Being a man is so hard...

Josh's hand tightens around my arm and for a

63

moment he's very still. Then he turns towards Jason again. Has *he* had enough? Is he gonna go for him?

"Look, Jason, I ain't got nothing against you. Or you against me. Weren't me that punched your teeth out, was it? Why don't we just leave the past and chill?"

Jason spits on the ground about an inch from Josh's boot. "Dream on, Wilson. You think a few sweet words make up for two front teeth? It's gonna take more than that to wipe the slate clean."

"Ain't nothing on my slate with you, Jason."

"You think not?" Jason's eyes dart behind us. "Well, I can square things with you any time I like. Easy as pie. Just remember that." With one final sneer he turns and leads his guys away.

I glance over my shoulder. West, Thiago, and Ed hurry up to us as the onlookers start to disperse.

"Jason causing trouble?"

"The usual." But Josh sounds absent-minded, seeming deep in thought.

Darryl stares at him, then speaks in a low voice. "Did that *mean* anything, Josh?"

He chews his lip for a moment. "I dunno. It could've just been a mean dig. He knows I loved my dad and it's not hard to guess that you two would love yours."

Belatedly, Jason's words sink in.

Such a shame when fathers get eaten, isn't it? Do they miss him terribly?

JOSHUA

Understanding blooms in Harry's eyes. "Was he talking about—?"

I shush him at just the same time as Darryl and reply softly, "I don't know, Harry. He might've just been being nasty. He's good at that."

"But you talked softly-softly after that."

"Sure. Just in case. Not that it helped."

"But you said...you said we didn't want anything to do with him. And he said something like, *you don't, huh*, like...almost like we should want it? Wasn't that a little odd?"

"Possibly. He does think he's something, though."

Darryl also looks like she's replaying the conversation in her mind. "At the end, he said that he could square things with you any time he liked, easy as pie. Could he mean by hurting Dad?"

I sigh, running a hand through my hair. "Again, *maybe*. Might just have been talking big, bowing out with a threat. But when he mentioned fathers...I admit, a horrible cold feeling went down my back. Because...well, it would kinda make a lotta sense, thinking about it."

"Yeah?" says West, glancing after Jason and his guys.

"Yeah," I say. "If Jason had snatched their dad, meaning to ransom him, but then they threw their lot in with *me*—d'you think he'd be in a hurry to give them—

and thus me—what I wanted? When *not* giving it to me is getting me in so much trouble? Oh, he was pretending to complain about it, but he was reveling in my fugitive status, you could see it."

I'm silent for a few more minutes as I think things through. It could all be nothing. It really, really could. But there were three separate moments in that conversation that coulda related to William Franklyn. And it would make a lotta sense.

"I think," I say at last, "that we need to put Jason Desmoines at the top of the list of suspects."

"We don't have a list of suspects," says Harry glumly.

"We do now," says Darryl.

DARRYL

Since Jason and his crew are much closer to their age, West and the others undertake to fish for info among their friends and acquaintances while we stick to the original plan of listening and chatting and making ourselves available for an approach from a kidnapper. The evidence against Jason is far too slim to stop the search with him. I think we're all distracted as we walk on our way. I certainly am. If, by the time we leave tomorrow, Jason is still our best lead, what do we do?

I've lost my enthusiasm for the fun of the fair, and I think Harry and Josh have too.

We can see the competition tents ahead when a loud claxon sounds and a red flare goes up from the closest part of the ring. In less than thirty seconds every child nearby is corralled inside a ring of bodies, the adults all facing outwards with their rifles, like muskoxen ready for a stand-off with wolves.

Several deep retorts echo from the ring—and there's a noticeable relaxation in tension.

"So, what's trying to get in?" asks Josh, slipping into teacher-mode the way he still does fairly often.

"Just piranha'saurs," Harry and I reply in unison. A piranha'saur gun has an especially distinctive sound.

A few more shots, and a green flare rises. The shoal's been driven off. The circles break up and activity resumes with barely a missed beat. We walk on our way, Harry fuming because a very old man with a long white beard all twined with feathers had tried to shove him into the center of the circle. At least, he simmers until he realizes he's amusing Josh.

"At his age, he mighta tried to shove *me* in, let alone you," smirks Josh.

Harry lets it go.

+

If one more old lady tells me that I need to marry Joshua, pronto... Does everyone think something's going on? Ugh. Having all these people think I'd hitch the plough in front of the tractor is maddening. But I guess Josh is right. God and Saint Des know the truth.

67

Unfortunately, we haven't picked up anything other than would-be helpful moral advice in the competition tents. Nothing about Dad, not a hint, though we've given everyone the perfect opening, telling how our Dad went missing, apparently eaten but no body left, even showing a photo of him. But if anyone knows anything, they aren't telling.

We keep on listening out as we get our evening meal and attend more storytelling—my favorite part of the evening is the story of Saint Desmond the Hermit and Beauty the raptor. Harry's *least* favorite thing is clearly watching West and Trudi sharing a sticky toffee apple, which *is* kinda cringeworthy. But before we know it we're back in the 'Vi and the fair is almost over. Just a half-day tomorrow, then everyone gets on the road at midday.

I stroke Kiko as he clings to my shoulder, trying to make it up to him for being left in the 'Vi all afternoon.

"So, what's on tomorrow?" asks Harry, sounding rather less interested in fair-stuff than he did at the beginning of the day. Guess he's wondering about Jason and Dad too. "Aren't there any shooting competitions?"

"Midsummer fair. A whole day of 'em. "

"So what do people do tomorrow?"

"Shop, mostly," say Josh. "Very few organized events, so it's the best time. But we'd better make sure we're ready to leave in good time."

He hesitates. Draws a deep breath. "Because I think...I think we need to follow Jason."

JOSHUA

It ain't a good idea. Anything that involves getting close to Jason out in the wilderness will be crazy-dangerous. Technicolor can't come with us. Not when all Jason needs is a photo of their vehicle with ours and he can drop them in it, big time—and the same goes for anyone who mighta helped us. Thanks to the city-folk, we've gotta do this alone. West and Ed are both ready to settle down, and Thiago can't go to prison right now, not with his mom so close to the end. Alone ain't a good idea and yet...I don't see what else we can do.

"That is...we can follow Jason," I say, "or we can give up and go to another state. I don't think there are any more options. West and the others can't do this for much longer."

"We can't give up!" says Harry.

Darryl shoots a glance at Harry, looking conflicted. Worried about his safety. But then her face firms. "We've got to try. If we need to do anything more—we can decide then."

Harry looks indignant. "We're not *giving up!*"

"I didn't say we were."

"We don't want to follow him from *here*," I say.

"He'll be taking all his camp-folk home, first. We want to get there before him, hide ourselves. Your dad won't be held in a camp—too many people would know; there'd be rumors by now. But if Jason heads right up into the mountains again, I wanna know where he goes."

Darryl nods. "So do I."

"Think Dad's there?" asks Harry.

"If he's not, then... Well." Then we'll probably never find him and it really may be time to give up.

+

In the morning, after Darryl's watch is over, we head out for a few hours of half-hearted shopping. Darryl wants a waistcoat like Trudi's—they sell them blank ready for decoration—Harry wants sweets, and I want to replenish our spices for cooking after Easter. We get everything, keeping our ears open but hearing nothing, before returning to the 'Vi to make ready for departure.

West reports only the usual nonspecific rumors of criminal activity that have swirled around the Desmoines clan for years. They're too well-off for the amount of hunting they seem to do, that's for sure. Seems like it's been a while since anyone saw Jason and his cousin Masey hunting together, either, which is a change.

As soon as the three red flares go up from the center of the fairground and the closing cacophony is over and

70

our gate opens, we pull away. Gateposts that aren't ready to move are never popular and we have twice the reason for speed. We need to get to Jason's camp in good time. He'll know that ground real well, so we'll have to be very careful how we position and camouflage the vehicle.

The last time I was outside Jason's camp, he threatened to shoot Uncle Z. I'm pretty sure he'd love an excuse to shoot me, too. I want to say, "let's forget it," but how can I? If it was my dad... I simply have to give them a chance to save him.

And I don't think we should delay. I can't stop worrying that after our little confrontation Jason might just go straight to wherever he's got their dad and kill him out of pure spite.

Assuming he's even got him. But we've got to assume that, because if he hasn't...we have nothing.

HARRY

If a winter of handicrafting was boring, it's nothing to this week outside Jason's camp. Boring and tense. Super-tense. Every minute of the day or night, one of us has to be up in the turret, peeping through the camo-netting at the camp, making sure Jason isn't either leaving or coming to attack us. He shouldn't be able to spot us. But Josh isn't taking any chances. And if we miss him leaving, all this stake-out will be for nothing.

I guess it's no worse than stake-out for culling purposes—except for the tension. Rogue carni'saurs don't come hunt you back—not if you stay in-Vi.

Josh says it's not uncommon for hunters to have some holiday around a fair time, yet only Jason's 'Vi returned, which is interesting. It brought back Masey's crew's families as well—we watched them all getting out, the vehicle was packed. So Masey went somewhere else straight after the fair. Josh reckons that suggests they've got something going that needs men almost all the time. No telling what it is. One kidnapped farmer wouldn't need a whole 'Vi-full of men. So they've either got a whole bunch of kidnapped folk or their main operation is something else.

Right now, I adjust the focus on my binos and slowly scan the camp. Nothing out of the ordinary. I lower the binos again. I'll see if a vehicle starts moving. When will they lead us to Dad?

My gut churns uncomfortably at the thought of Dad, the way it has all week. I can't stop thinking how we've been having fun with Josh for almost a year—okay, getting cold, tired, wet, working to the bone, scared of getting caught and, honestly, I'm not quite as sold on hunter-life as Darryl is but, still, basically having a fairly good time—while Dad has been a prisoner. Do they hurt him? Do they feed him and treat him well, like a piece of valuable livestock?

Jason was so *nasty*. Meeting him really brought it

home to me just how bad things could've been for Dad. While we've been living our lives and wondering whether to give up and slope off out-state... I feel horrible.

We've *got to* save him.

First, we need to find him.

Come on, Jason. Surely you need to go relieve Masey soon?

DARRYL

I wake with a start as my bed lurches. What the—? Oh, engine's running, we're underway. Is Jason on the move at last? I've been napping, still fully dressed in my day clothes, ready for the first nightshift. The constant watch is grueling, even with three of us.

Grabbing my rifle, I quickly slide down from my berth, Kiko following. The living area shutters are closed for travel but I duck into the cab without turning the lights on because I realize it's dark outside. We don't even have headlights on! Bright moonlight illuminates boulders and small trees as we inch along, but it's barely enough visibility to be safe.

"We're driving at night? With no lights?"

"Just getting out of sight of the camp," says Josh. "Jason left soon after you turned in. If we can get clear tonight without being seen, we can pick up his trail first thing in the morning. You can bet we're not going far, like this."

Jason's out here. Oh boy. Unease curdles my gut. It's really happening. We're tracking a potentially dangerous criminal into the wilderness. A whole HabVi of potential criminals. This is *not* a good idea.

But what other choice do we have?

HARRY

The deeper we get into the mountains, the more cautiously we advance. The last thing we need is to stumble on Jason and get ourselves seen. The snow was showing signs of melting down near Jason's camp, but it's still holding up here and that's doing us a big favor. We can drive much higher up the valley side, simply following the tracks of Jason's 'Vi with binos, instead of getting down to the altitude they're using and risking running into them at close quarters. Josh fixed brushes behind our rear tires to reduce the visibility of our own tracks—at least from a distance. Clearly, with wind and fresh snowfalls usually obscuring tracks within hours or days, Jason doesn't see the need.

We've left all the camo netting and snow sheets in place over the 'Vi, except for the windshield. The glint off that could still give us away, but the rest of us is pretty inconspicuous and it's not safe driving on this terrain without good visibility.

Right now, Josh is at the wheel and I'm up in the

turret, on watch. Darryl's grabbing some sleep. We've been following Jason for two days and Josh refuses to allow all of us to be asleep at the same time.

"If Jason spots us," he said firmly, the first evening, "he can't do nothing unless he catches us. We keep someone on watch all the time."

Peering ahead, I squint through the dangling camo net that still shields the turret windows, trying to make out... A flash...more quartz in the mountainside? Or... I hit the intercom button. "Josh, stop!"

Even as the 'Vi slows to a halt I'm raising one of the windows a fraction and releasing the cord to allow the camo net to slide down over our windshield.

"What is it?" Josh asks.

"A vehicle. Maybe."

By the time I've got my binos focused on the object, he's climbing up into the turret.

"It's a 'Vi," I tell him. "But not Jason's."

Josh locates the vehicle with his own binos and nods. "It's Masey. On his way back. We must be nearly there."

"Will he see us?"

Josh glances around, and I'm experienced enough by now that I know what he's looking at. Mixed landscape behind and around us, very similar colors to our camouflage. "I doubt it. Best thing we can do is not move a muscle. They're a lot lower down than we are, they won't be looking up here much."

Déjà vu. Can't have been that far from here that we hid from Jason in the fall, right? We could have followed him then, if we'd known. Or maybe not. Unless I've got my directions mixed up, I think he was heading toward his camp that time, the way Masey is now.

Josh continues to track the oncoming HabVi, frowning as he watches it trundling closer and closer. He and Darryl are both super-tense about all this, like they're *this close* to giving up on the whole thing.

No, I won't let them, *I won't.* We have to save Dad!

JOSHUA

"So, do you want the good news or the bad news?" I say, as I finish inspecting Jason's secret camp through my telescopic sights.

We've got the 'Vi into a real good position, with only the tip of the heavily camouflaged turret peeping over the crags, giving us a good view of the camp in the bottom of the valley but keeping us well screened from heat sensors. The place we're parked—high up on the mountain—is only accessible through a series of twisting ravines. I scouted on foot to find it and had Darryl drive the 'Vi in once darkness had fallen last night, while I led the way. The chances of anyone in a vehicle finding us here are very slim indeed. There's even a partial overhang in the cliff above, reducing the chances of a drone getting a look at us.

"Bad news," says Darryl grimly, just as Harry says, "Good news."

"Bad news is, that place is so heavily camouflaged if it weren't for the straight lines of the fence posts it would practically be invisible. The bunkhouse is fairly clear, but no telling what else is down there. Two large barns and a smaller place, I'd say. But it's hard to be certain."

"Two large barns?" Darryl focuses our best binos, though they're not as good as my gun sights. "I guess that slight curve—if it is a curve—could be a camouflaged roof. But what do kidnappers need large barns for?"

"The more I look at that place, the more I suspect kidnapping ain't their main operation. Maybe they were going through a lean patch when they decided to grab him for some quick cash."

Darryl's face tenses. "In that scenario, they probably didn't keep him this long, right?"

"Unless Jason then decided to keep him as something to hold over me. You never know, his hate might actually have worked in our favor."

"I guess."

"Only other possibility is that West is right and there's something more to it. Mebbe your dad somehow found out about them or...something else."

Harry makes a face. "Also not good! They probably

did just kill him, in that case, and we've been chasing a wish-dream all year."

I grimace, but don't bother to deny it.

"But we're miles from the farm, so it's not likely, right? What do you think that place is, anyway?" demands Harry.

I sigh. "Heck, I dunno, Harry. Something very illegal, plain as day, 'cause you don't site a legitimate business way up here and cam it up like that. But what? Could be anything."

"We're gonna find out, right? We're gonna go down there and find Dad? Tonight?"

Darryl's eyes dart from Harry to me, her face tenser than ever.

"I guess that's what we need to decide," I say quietly.

DARRYL

"We've come this far!" bursts out Harry. "This is the whole reason we came, right? We didn't just come to *look* at the place. What good will that do? We've gotta go in there and get Dad out!"

Josh says nothing. He just settles back into a seat, leans back and folds his arms. Eventually, he says, in a very measured way, "I don't see any way to get your dad other than going in there, it's true."

"Ransom?" I say, hearing the pleading in my voice.

I just don't want Harry—or Josh—to get hurt!

Josh is silent for a while, clearly mulling this over. He looks a little sick. "I think...I just...can't shake the feeling that if we open talks with Jason—even assuming we can find some way to do it without him killing or capturing us—I just have this feeling it's gonna end with him chucking us a bag and laughing in our faces. And your dad's head will be in the bag."

My stomach churns, and Harry's face takes on a green tinge.

"Negotiations could be very, very dangerous for your dad," says Josh. "And trying to open negotiations would be very, very dangerous for us."

"And if we go down there..."

"That's a right rex rodeo too."

I sink down in a seat as well, pulling at my braid, then distractedly stroking Kiko as he flutters into my lap. Heck, what do we do? We've been so, so careful to make sure Jason doesn't know we're here. The moment we try to approach him...well, we couldn't do it here. Then he'd know we knew about...

My heart sinks. "We'd have to try and speak to him back at his home camp, right? But will he guess we followed him? I mean, what he said at the fair, it wasn't enough to be sure."

"We could make out we were just *wondering* if he had him," says Harry. "And offer enough money to hook him?"

Josh frowns, his eyes going to the window again. "Problem is," he says slowly, "without knowing what that place is down there, we don't know what counts as 'enough money' to hook Jason. He could be making a modest supplementary income growing some forbidden but relatively harmless crop—or at the other end of the scale, he could be into something really, really lucrative. If it's the latter, he'll laugh at our offer and kill us just in case we do know anything about his operation."

"If it's the latter, why did he take Dad?" I say. "Back to that again. Surely it's something less serious?"

"We're going in circles," says Harry. "Big crime, Dad's probably dead; little crime, maybe he's alive, right?"

"Yeah," says Josh. "*Oh, hello, Kiko.*" He gives the little quadravian some absent-minded attention.

"Then let's forget big crime. Big crime, we can't do anything! Let's assume it's small crime. Is it better to negotiate or sneak in? There's only four guys down there, right?"

"One of whom wants to shoot Josh," I say. "Honestly, the thought of giving him this good an excuse does freak me out."

"Forget about me specifically," says Josh. "You two have to accept that if we go down there and get caught, we'll likely all be killed." He stares at me, his brows drawn together, like he's considering adding something else specific about me, but he doesn't. Well, I'm not an idiot; he doesn't need to say it.

My stomach vibrating uncomfortably, I toss my braid over my shoulder, then rest my elbows on my knees and my chin on my hands. "Maybe Harry should stay here," I say at last.

Does that mean I think we should go in? Ransom just seems so dodgy. We'd have to go off and contact Uncle Mau before we could even offer any money; it's all so uncertain. And what if it's precisely what Jason's waiting for, so he can have his moment of twisted triumph?

"I'm *coming!*" says Harry.

I open my mouth, but he cuts me off.

"You've both been treating me like a man for a year! You can't just treat me like a kid again, now when it really matters!"

"We didn't let you compete in the rodeo," says Josh dryly.

"I didn't see you or Darryl competing, either. That was common sense, not *age.*"

It was your age, I almost say, but don't bother. "Josh, what was the good news?"

"Right, the *good news* is that fence down there is to keep out wildlife, not people. Ain't a proper camp fence, it's barely more than a large portable set-up. No real need for anything more, I suppose. The isolation will protect against humans and who wants to drag

81

heavy fencing equipment right up here? Although, if those *are* big barns down there, they already brought the parts for those. Maybe..." He rises to stare down at the camp for another moment. "Huh, of course."

"What?" I ask.

"We came expecting a criminal enterprise, so that's what we saw. But a casual observer, if they notice the place at all, will just see that bunkhouse and that very non-permanent-looking fence and assume it's a temporary hunting camp."

"And the barns?"

"We're not even sure they're there, and we've been staring at it for an hour. From a distance someone could easily miss them. Just see a temporary camp, decide they don't want the trouble of going down there and trying to move the hunters on—doubt Jason owns that land—and go straight on their way. Jason kills two birds with one stone with that basic fence—adds a layer of more subtle camouflage and saves a lotta work and costs."

"But we could get through it okay?" I check.

"Sure."

"So we can get in, and there are only four guys to avoid. So if we snuck in at night—"

"*Might* be only four guys," says Josh. "Jason's 'Vi is four-men, Masey is three strong and hopefully all three just left with him. That doesn't mean there ain't one or two or even more guys who stay up here longer term."

"How likely is that?"

Josh shrugs. "Since Jason and Masey keep swapping shifts, unlikely. But we can't know."

"Do you think they keep a watch?"

"Way out here? No."

"Huh. You know, I'm actually starting to think sneaking in and taking a look around might be safer than trying ransom."

"Yeah." Josh speaks slowly. "I'm kinda coming round to that way of thinking too."

HARRY

My heart leaps. Are we gonna do it?

Josh is eyeing me again. "Ideally, we need one person back here to provide cover."

My heart plummets again. Then I frown, swinging around to look out of the window. "Oh, come off it, Josh, our entire approach is hidden behind the crags, the whole mile down the mountain. The only part we can see is the valley bottom and the camp, which is way out of effective range. It's not worth leaving one person here and I'm not falling for it!"

Josh's gaze goes steely. "If I say you're staying here, then you're staying here."

My mouth opens to announce that if they try to leave me behind I'll just follow on behind them, but I shut it again just in time. I'm getting wise to hunter-ways, now. To Josh's little tests. Children disobey—and that's why they don't go on dangerous raids. "Of course," I manage. "You're the boss."

A hint of a smile touches Josh's tense mouth, as though he knows the farmer boy is playing him at his own game, but he simply glances at Darryl. "Unfortunately, he's right. We've no choice but to keep the 'Vi parked here and hidden, but it means we ain't gonna have cover."

Uh-oh, I know what that glance means. Far as I'm concerned, he's gonna leave it up to my big sis.

Darryl drags her hands down her face. "Ugh, this whole thing is so dangerous. What happens if Harry stays here and Jason catches us two?"

"Then after whatever cut-off time we give him, Harry has to try to navigate the 'Vi back out of here, solo, with Jason and all his guys looking all over for it."

"And his chances?"

"Not great. They'll have a drone and heat sensors and they know the area better."

"Then..." Darryl gives a huge sigh. "Then I guess he probably might as well come with us."

Yes!

Josh eyes Darryl again. "Maybe...maybe *Harry and I* should go down there and you—"

Darryl shoots down this suggestion with the kinda glare that makes Josh raise his hands in immediate surrender. Guess we're all going. By tomorrow morning, will we have rescued Dad?

I try not to jiggle up and down like a little kid.

"What do we need to do?" I ask.

JOSHUA

The sky is clouded, which means moonlight will vary between sporadic to none at all, so we set off in the twilight to give us the best chance of making it down to the valley floor without breaking an ankle.

"Make sure you memorize the route as best you can," I remind them. "We'll be coming back up in the dark—we hope."

They nod silently. No need to go over everything again. We all know the plan. Getting back to the 'Vi tonight and getting gone is obviously far, far preferable but groping our way back up an entire mountain in pitch darkness may simply be impossible and showing a light suicidal, in which case we'll get out of sight of the camp and find a crack to tuck ourselves in until daylight.

"Stay alert," I add, as I start moving. "Don't forget Jason and Co. ain't the only dangerous critters out here."

Trekking about out-Vi with no cover at all. Just the first on the list of risks we're running tonight.

We're only carrying very limited weapons. Heck, was that a hard decision. We argued ourselves in circles. Weapons are good for wildlife—*except* we can't fire them without giving ourselves away—but might be good if we got caught, too. Or might just get us shot on sight. And might clink against pretty much anything. The way sound carries at night, one *chink*, and we're caught. You can't climb easily, can't squeeze through gaps quickly, everything is restricted if you have a large chunk of metal dangling from your body. The reason why hunters routinely leave rifles behind for any out-Vi activity that doesn't definitely need one.

In the end, we decided to go with the tried and tested reasoning and not take them. The three of us with our sturdy sticks, along with my frights—noise-maker disabled—have a decent chance of scaring off a single pair of deinons or a pack of velociraptors, which is all we're likely to meet until we get right down to the valley floor. We each have a flare pistol to use as a close-range weapon of last resort, but the moment we fire so much as a single shot our chances of getting away drop to next to nothing.

I set a steady pace, moving carefully, especially over loose snow that might slide—or put up snowdust into the air that could be visible from below. We packed light, so we can move fast. I have the fence tools and each of us has a thermal survival blanket—one of those tiny little folded squares of silver foil, the lightest and smallest type—along with a handful of sachets of blood clotter for first aid use, our knives, of course, and little else.

We've set up auto-send messages to West and to Maurice Carr that will go if we don't cancel them by midday tomorrow, telling them what we've done, requesting that they move immediately to approach Jason and try to secure our freedom. I daresay Maurice would offer him money and Technicolor the business end of their rifles. One or other approach might work—assuming we're still alive to be rescued. It's the only real contingency plan we could come up with.

The idea is to be super stealthy. In and out. A lot will depend on what condition their dad's in, though, if he is there.

We're finally nearing the bottom of the slope. I pause beside a suitable bush so we can cut a few branches to use for scentCam. We want to wait until at least midnight, if not later, when Jason and his guys should be fast asleep.

Once there's no terrain between us and the camp that will be too dangerous to negotiate in the dark, we pile into a crack in the cliff and arrange our scentCam in front of us, huddling together for warmth. We don't want to get those glittery blankets out unless we absolutely have to. They're almost impossible to fold up small again and they rustle fit to wake the dead. They really are for emergencies.

Fortunately, although the temperature still hovers around freezing, the cloud cover means it won't drop much further as the darkness deepens and there's still no wind to speak of—bad for wiping out our tracks but good for windchill factor. We've dressed suitably, we'll be fine. Chilly, but fine.

Now, there's nothing to do but sit and think about all the things that could go wrong. *Outage,* I didn't want to do this. I really didn't. I'm so afraid of them getting hurt. I want Harry safe because he really is barely a man, though he tries so hard, and Darryl because... because I can't even bear the thought of Jason getting a'hold of her. I even tried to persuade them to just let me come down and scout it out by myself, but they wouldn't hear of it.

It's our dad.

And it's true. At the end of the day, however worried I am about their safety, it's their dad. And they have a right to try and save him.

DARRYL

"Okay, here goes." I barely catch Josh's soft words.

It's the deep of the night; the camp is silent and dark. We've crept up to the fence and now we're all lying in the snow, hidden in the undergrowth that's been allowed to grow quite close, no doubt for extra concealment.

Josh has pulled out the set of leads and insulated supports that he prepared and is about to bypass the

88

bottom fence wire so we can remove a section. He even brought the splicer so we can repair it when we leave. That way, they'll probably each assume it's an old repair made by one of the others—so long as the wind or some fresh snowfall gets rid of our tracks before they notice them.

I sense Josh's arms moving, catch a pinprick of red light from the adjustable beam of his flashlight as he makes sure he doesn't touch the fence by accident. Moments later, I hear the snick of wire being cut. Once. Twice. I lie motionless, pressed to the ground, my heart hammering in my chest as I wait for an alarm, for shouting, for doors flying open...

Nothing. Josh's trick worked. The fence controller hasn't noticed that part of the current is now being routed through our insulated addition.

"Let's go," breathes Josh. "Keep very low, there's not much space."

He shines the red flashlight on the wires above as we each crawl through so he can make sure we're not about to get zapped, then we're on our feet, looking around.

We move with slow strides over the hard-packed areas, to reduce the crunching of snow under our feet, trying to walk on top of tracks that are already there. In the softer drifts around the camp edges we can move much faster without noise, but we avoid those as much as possible because the fresh tracks will stand out. The snow is a real liability for this sort of thing. We could spend time brushing them away behind us but it's not going to fool experienced trackers and will take too long. We just have to hope for wind or snow before morning.

Josh was right. Two big barns loom to the right. They're semicircular, roofed in flexi-corrugated metal that was probably brought here in huge rolls, simple to transport, the curved shape easy to blend into the landscape. The smaller, grey-green but otherwise un-camouflaged, building is almost certainly living accom-modation. A separate toilet stands just outside the back door. There's one storage shed—not locked. We check inside anyway. Fence maintenance equipment. And a larger shed.

Josh peers through the window, shining his flash-light. "That's for butchering a whole animal," he says. Then frowns.

I guess I know what he's thinking. What if this whole place actually *is* just a hunting camp, with a butchery like on a farm, all set up to allow them to hunt more efficiently? Cammed up simply because they don't own the land it's built on, maybe? No, those barns don't fit with that.

The accommodation block is one of the obvious places for a prisoner to be held, so we creep up to the nearest window. Rough curtains, carelessly drawn. Easy to see in. A light glows inside, over the back door that leads out to the privy, dimly illuminating the interior. Hooks holding outdoor coats and a row of boots are visible in the corner by the door. In the next corner are the cooking facilities. Is it...yes, it's all one room, a basic bunkhouse, like Josh predicted. A seating area takes up the third corner. And four bunk beds in the fourth. All four occupied. Dad's not in there.

Relief and disappointment collide. If he'd been here then we'd have found him, but then we'd have to hold up Jason and his guys with the flare pistols, at least long enough to take their rifles.

But Dad's not there.

It is only the four guys, though. That's good.

Josh tugs my sleeve, drawing me towards the barns. Huge, we see, as we get close to them. What are they *growing* in there?

A few small access doors dot the end walls, but these ones are locked. The main barn doors in the center of each end of the building are too large to open quietly, but we have to try them. Locked too. This part of the camp is very secure.

Josh tugs my sleeve again, pointing up. A ladder gives quick access to the camouflaged roof, so it can be used as a makeshift turret in the event of a breach, no doubt. The barn sides are steep at the bottom part of the curve — too steep for anything to climb — but fairly flat on top. And there'll be access from inside the barn as well, I bet.

91

We climb as quietly as we can, our ice-encrusted soles slipping on the round metal rungs. But we make it safely to the top. Dodging fake bushes and camonetting, we open the nearest roof hatch. I climb onto the ladder and start down it, Harry following. Josh comes last, pausing to pull the hatch to behind us. Partway down, my foot slides off the rung while I'm moving my handgrip—I grab for a rung but they're wet and the next second I'm falling.

Smack. I manage to land on my feet, grabbing the ladder for support. *Outage,* that jarred my whole body.

"Darryl?" Harry hisses, climbing down quickly.

"I'm fine," I whisper, as he joins me on the floor.

I put my red flashlight on at the lowest setting, the aperture at its narrowest. The floor under us is made of immensely strong metal bars. Essentially mesh, but on a massive scale. It slopes downwards, towards heavy, wide-spaced metal bars that remind me of a handling barn at home on the farm, but with a half-yard gap at the bottom. I was expecting grow lamps or...or maybe some kind of packing facility.

I step closer and shine the flashlight through the bars. It's...a collection tray of some kind. And there are eggs there. Big 'saur eggs, over fifteen inches long. In the red light, I can't tell the color, but they're larger than Edmo eggs.

Faint scuffs approach as Josh comes quickly down the ladder. "Heck, you two, *wait up!*" he breathes, as he steps off the bottom. "Can't you *smell* the—"

"Josh," Harry interrupts him. "What sort of eggs are these?"

Josh barely glances towards them—then goes motionless. "We're on the wrong side of the—" He breaks off. "Light out. *Don't move.*"

I click the flashlight off, sensing Harry go rigid beside me. We stand in complete silence. I can almost hear Josh *listening*.

Deep breathing sounds come from around the barn. A lot of them. Including...including from just a few feet away from us. Livestock. *Large* stock. *The wrong side of the bars*, Josh was going to say. We've come down right into one of the actual pens. Not a good idea. Fortunately...

"She's asleep," breathes Josh. "Get into that egg tray. Very, very quietly."

"*What's* asleep?" asks Harry.

"*Just move.*"

Heck. What *is* in here with us?

Carefully, by feel, I find the bottom of the bars and ease myself under them, through the gap. The eggs are strong enough I could jump up and down on one, no problem, just like an Edmo egg, so there's no risk of damaging them. I'm guessing they aren't Edmo eggs, though. Josh would've simply said so.

Only once we're all three in the egg tray does Josh put his flashlight on.

"What is this place, Josh?" I whisper.

"This," says Josh, aiming the light into the pen, where the darkness swallows the feeble red beam. "Is an illegal rex battery farm." He opens the aperture wider and the beam of light illuminates the head of a sleeping she-rex a few feet from the foot of the ladder.

Harry gasps and flinches back against the wall of the egg tray, making a dull clang as his flashlight strikes the metal.

"Shhh!" Josh hisses.

I stare at the she-rex, stunned. She can barely lie down in the pen, it's so small. She's curled around in a hunched-up half-moon shape, the open section facing us, which is the only reason we didn't step on her. Her bones show, pushing against her skin. She looks desperately unhealthy.

I put my own flashlight on again, open the aperture wider and shine it all around the barn. The whole thing is divided into these tiny—for the size of the stock—pens. Two long alleys of them. The egg trays run along the outer walls. Along the center is the feed alley. They must butcher meat on site in quantity and dump it along there for the she-rex to eat.

"This is horrible. I didn't think there had been battery farms for decades."

"I said an *illegal* battery farm."

"The rex look terrible," says Harry, shining his flashlight from pen to pen, picking out each slumbering animal in turn.

"They're probably well-fed, but they give them non-stop hormones and stimulants to keep them laying constantly. She-rex only lay one clutch a year, naturally."

"Never mind that!" Harry's whisper is a little too loud. "Dad's *not here*!"

"We need to check the other barn," I say.

Josh winces. "Yeah, obviously we will but...Darryl, this is *huge* money, this operation. There are only three legal, licensed rex farms in the country, and only two of them are egg production. You know how much rex eggs go for on the black market. No way they took your dad because they needed a little extra pocket money."

I swallow, hard, my stomach dropping. Which means...he found something out and they just killed him?

No. We have to check. What if they grabbed him to kill him and then stuff happened fast enough that Jason found out we were with Josh, and...it's possible, right?

"Come on." My voice wobbles, no matter how hard I try to stop it. "Let's check the other barn."

"Okay," says Josh. "Let's get back to the ladder."

HARRY

"You're kidding?" I say.

Josh shakes his head. "I don't see any other way out

of these egg trays. We're standing on a conveyer belt, but it's accessed from one of those small doors we tried, which are locked from outside. Actually, head straight on through the pen and climb out into the center aisle. I'm pretty sure there's another ladder there and it will be safer to go up that one in case someone slips again. Turn your flashlights right down and remember, we're plastered in scentBlock so if she wakes, just stand still."

I gulp. Darryl takes a deep breath. Josh is already slipping under the bars and padding across the pen, silent as a hunting wolf and about as concerned. Darryl ducks very carefully and follows. *Outage!* Under I go. I try to imitate their stealthy glide, feeling like a lumbering armadillion.

The she-rex stirs slightly, head shifting, nostrils flaring. I stand rigid, trying not to gasp for breath. But her eyelids don't stir, and soon she's sleeping peacefully again. Or exhaustedly. Dreaming of open plains, of juicy herds of iguanodons? No, she was probably raised in captivity. She's never known anything but this tiny, dark pen, with cold, pre-cut meat and Jason and his men shouting at her. Scorch marks mar her hide from overuse of electric prods, and her crest feathers are thin and bedraggled. Poor creature.

Still, I'm really glad once I've managed to climb over her tail without touching it and made it through the bars into the feed alley, away from her. Feed alley...a crunched up Edmo leg bone lies just beside me, though the troughs are clean, like they're scrubbed and sanitized regularly. But, yeah...I climb quickly from the food trough and get out of grabbing distance.

Josh is already pointing to another ladder. "There it is."

It goes up from beside some sort of main control panel, by the barn doors at the bunkhouse end. Josh waves us on up the ladder, still eyeing the she-rex. Only as I get close to him do I register his tense shoulders and smoldering eyes. I've never seen him really angry before. Yeah, I agree, but I'm eager to be gone. I start climbing.

Darryl moves to get on the ladder, then pauses as Josh starts touching the control screen, muttering something about every creature deserving to see the sky at least once. She focuses the beam of her flashlight high up over the gates of the individual pens. "Josh? Those are flashing lights. If they put those up, they won't have missed off the sirens, not on rex pens. Don't do it."

Don't do what? *Outage*, is he gonna let them *out*? Oh man, but that would serve Jason right when he came in here in the morning!

Josh glances at Darryl and me, taps the screen some more, then turns away from the controls with a regretful shake of his head. "Sorry, ladies, you'll have to take your chances," he murmurs. "My own family comes first."

I release the breath I didn't realize I was holding.

97

'Cause there's no *way* we'd have got away with *that* without waking Jason and Co. We might as well knock on the door of the bunkhouse and tell them we're here!

Soon we're back on the roof and Josh is quietly closing the hatch behind us.

One barn left. One more chance.

One barn and we can get out of here...

DARRYL

"Remember that weird blocky table in the bunkhouse," I murmur, as we creep across the roof of the second barn, this time heading for the center hatch.

"Incubator," says Josh. "They breed their own replacements."

I nod. "Exactly what I was going to say."

"Keep it in there; let it help heat the place. Makes sense."

"Until baby rex crawl out one morning and eat your boots. Or your *feet*," mutters Harry.

"Nah, they can't get out," says Josh, opening the hatch.

Center ladder or not, we turn our flashlights to max and take a good hard look from the roof this time.

"This is a young stock barn," says Josh. "Look"—he points along the pens in turn with the beam—"Hatchlings, nestlings, and different ages of juveniles. That penful by the door look almost kill weight."

"Kill weight?" queries Harry.

"The quality females in that other pen will be the replacements. The rest are all for meat. Some people will eat anything, if it's rare enough." He hesitates. "I'm not sure there's much point going down there."

"There's some sort of storeroom at the far end, look!" says Harry. "We've got to check it, Josh!"

"Then we will have checked everywhere," I say quietly.

Josh nods. "Okay. Let's be quick."

I manage not to fall off this ladder, and soon we're all standing in the aisle. The storeroom's right by the control panel. Did we miss a storeroom in the other barn? No, it was pens all through. The door opens, it's not locked. Probably 'cause it is just a storeroom. Huge tubs of supplements, shovels, a broom. Not much junk. Despite the poor treatment of the stock, it's quite a professional set-up.

But no Dad. My heart sinks lower. I close the door and move toward the ladder. Josh is messing with this control screen too. What's he *doing*?

Light floods the barn as the roof lights blaze into life. For a second I think Josh is responsible—then a harsh voice snaps, "Get your hands up."

I can barely see in the sudden glare, but I think Josh taps the controls twice, screening the movement with his body, before putting his hands out and up, clearly visible. Reluctantly, still squinting as I try to see, I do the same.

"And you, kid," snaps the voice.

"Harry, do it," says Josh in a low voice.

Thank God, Harry obeys.

"Now, turn around, all of you, nice and slow."

We obey. My eyes are starting to adjust slightly, and I make out a Jason-clan-looking guy standing there, pointing a rifle our way. I think he was at the fair, standing right next to Jason. Only one man. Can we overpower him, somehow?

The young rex are lumbering to their feet, snapping and snarling at each other in their packed communal pens, grumpy to be woken by the unexpected light, but the guy ignores them, too busy staring at Josh.

"*Wilson?* What the *short-circuiting fences*—? *Misfire*, you've taken your bleeding-heart-save-the-dinos crap too far this time, boy. You think you can just sneak in here and mess with our rexes? Ooh, Jason's gonna skin you alive, you bet'ya he is." His eyes shift to me and his astonishment deepens. "And you *brought your little mare* with you? What the heck, Wilson? Don't like her that much, after all?"

His surprise gives way to a leer as his eyes run over me again. "Huh, y'know, Wilson, we've just come on shift and it don't half get boring out here. I reckon you've done us a big favor."

"Shut your mouth," snaps Harry.

The guy just snorts. "*You'll* make a nice morsel for

100

the juveniles." He jerks the rifle. "Step a little to your left, go on..."

Harry shoots a glance that way, but the only thing to his left is the feed trough. A couple of juvenile rex stare into it as though wondering if the light means that an early breakfast is coming their way. The color drains from Harry's cheeks and my fists clench.

"Go on," smirks the guy. "Step down into there, boy, or I'll put a bullet in your leg and watch you topple in."

We're gonna have to rush the creep...

"Think Jason will be happy with you having all the fun by your lonesome, Caleb?" says Josh, sounding tense but surprisingly calm.

Caleb screws up his face in disgust. "Argh, always have to be right, don't you, Wilson? Fine, let's go see how Jason likes being woken up to deal with you three. Sure you wouldn't all rather jump into that trough? No?" He twitches the rifle—just a normal one, not a rex-gun, not that it makes any difference when either will kill us. "Fine, more fool you. Walk to that door, there. The little one."

I shoot a look at Josh. Does he have a plan? How did this guy catch on to us? Visited the outhouse and saw our tracks, most likely. Darn snow.

Josh turns slowly towards the door, so I do too.

My heart almost jolts from my body as claxons sound up and down the length of the barn. I glance up.

The warning lights flash on almost every pen as the gates begin to slide open.

Josh spins around to face Caleb, his hands still held high and harmless. "Hey man, *what the heck are you doing?*" he yells. "Are you *mad?*"

Caleb's got his rifle trained on Josh, finger on the trigger like he's about to fire, but his mouth falls open as though he was about to shout the exact same thing at Josh.

"*Do something!*" shouts Josh, sounding surprisingly alarmed for someone who insists rex are nothing to worry about if you just know how to stand still properly.

A juvenile is already pushing its head through the steadily increasing gap of the nearest pen entrance, peering up and down the aisle curiously. Most interesting thing that's ever happened in its entire life, most likely.

Caleb moves towards the control panel, then his eyes dart to the three of us. He'll have to come close... His eyes shift to the wall behind us. He takes another step, glances at us again—we watch, tensely, waiting— the juvenile begins to move out of the pen—he swears, turns and sprints down the aisle.

"Hey, don't *run*, you fool!" yells Josh, and I think he means it, this time. He glances immediately at me and Harry. "*Don't* move."

Harry stands rigid, his shoulders tense. "You

think?" he mutters, as the first juvenile steps right out, lowering its head and sniffing around, crest feathers flaring. More follow, blocking our view of Caleb, whose yells suddenly ring out, loud and ominous. His rifle fires twice, not that that will help him much.

I concentrate on standing still as the juveniles spill from the pens, suddenly glad of every minute of the ruthless motion training Josh put us through months ago. He was right. Practice is nothing like keeping still when real rex are feet away. Rex muscles ripple under green-brown hide and their scent fills my nose. No way will I fail to recognize it in future. The ground trembles slightly as their feet shuffle and thud. *Just stand still, Darryl.*

Stand still, Harry...

"*Misfire*," mutters Josh. "Too many!"

He's right about that. The rex are getting closer and closer, every last one trying to pack out into the aisle, except the smallest ones, which remain shut in their pens. It soon won't matter if they notice we're edible or not, we're about to get knocked down or crushed. Josh turns — slowly — and lifts three long electric stock prods from the wall behind the control screen, handing one to each of us. Moving slow, all the time. Slow is less interesting.

"Here. Darryl, help me keep them back. Harry, start climbing that ladder."

The prods are what Caleb was after, aren't they?

103

But he knew if he came for them we'd jump him. There are probably more at the other end of the barn. Did he reach them? He's stopped yelling—I think—the rex are stomping and growling and snarling all around, filling my ears with their racket. Must've been at least ten in each pen, could be forty to fifty loose. I hold the prod out in front of me, occasionally pressing the button to make it spark. So far, the rex are keeping a little distance from us humans. Probably haven't had many positive experiences with our kind.

"Darryl, go." Harry's out the way, so Josh shifts to shield the ladder as much as he can by himself.

Someone has to go last, there's no point arguing and causing a delay. I get on the ladder and climb as fast as I can, one-handed because I'm still gripping the prod. I really don't want to let go of that right now.

"Darryl!"

Ugh! Hooking an arm through the bars, I get the prod pointing the right way just in time, jabbing at the juvenile's nose as it thrusts it towards me. Just curious, I think, but I'm not playing around with something that size. Might be curious what I taste like. It recoils before the prod can touch it. Yep, they know what the prods are, poor things.

"Sorry," I mutter, hurrying up the ladder, though I didn't actually zap it. I can hear Josh coming up behind me, thank God.

And then, *thank God, thank God*, we're all on the

roof. Alive and intact.

"Caleb?" A voice is yelling. "Caleb, where you at? What's going on?"

"*Jason*," whispers Josh, creeping to the front of the barn roof and peeping past a fake bush, then looking straight down. Harry and I join him.

Jason crouches with another man against the barn wall below us, as though they're waiting for something. Light from the bunkhouse windows reflects off the rifles in their hands.

"It sounds like some of the juveniles are loose," says the other man. Unlike Caleb, they stay very still in the shadows, though their voices carry in the night silence. From ground level they'd be almost invisible.

"Barn doors are still shut at this end. They may just be loose inside. Let's worry about them when we know what's going on."

Nuh-ur, I definitely saw the barn doors at the *far* end opening, though the juveniles seemed slow to go right outside, into the night. Too unfamiliar.

A third man creeps up and crouches beside them. "Fence has been cut. There're footprints all around. One man and two...well, I'd almost say a young woman and a lad, but I guess it's probably two lads. No one would bring a woman here."

"Who *would* come here, period?" snarls Jason. "Must be someone trying to take over our operation."

"Or just steal some rex eggs?" suggests the guy who

105

was waiting with Jason.

"More fool them. Shoot on sight. They don't leave here alive to tell tales. Nashoba, you and Gerry make a foot patrol. Just keep your eyes peeled for those juveniles. I'll get on top of the egg barn and cover you, make sure they don't slip back through the fence, neither. And *don't* shoot Caleb by accident. He may be an idiot, but he's my brother and you ain't."

"Gotcha."

"Yes, boss."

"Cover me till I get to the barn..."

Joshua draws back from the edge as Jason darts towards the egg barn, making use of the other buildings for cover along the way. The moon is half-out and nothing's as dark as it was before.

Josh's eyes are wide; I've never seen him so frantic. "We've gotta get out of here, *now*. Moment Jason gets on top of that barn, he sees us, or at best we're pinned down and can't go nowhere!"

"But *how*—?" Harry's voice quivers as hard as my innards.

Josh is right, we've *got* to go. But between three—maybe four—hostile guys, who're going to shoot on sight, and a hoard of juvenile rex... *How?*

Josh stares at the electric prods in our hands, as though having an idea he doesn't like much. "Oh, *misfire*." He dashes back across the barn roof, heading for the other end. We follow.

"There they are," he murmurs, looking down. He looks out. "And there's the fence."

Not far below us, juveniles spill out of the barn a little way, peering into the darkness, crest feathers flaring as curiosity wars with wariness. About thirty feet away is the fence on the opposite side of the camp from where we came in.

"Now I'm really wishing you'd both had a go at the rodeo," mutters Josh.

"What?" says Harry. My stomach clenches.

Josh shoots a glance at the egg barn. Jason must be starting up the ladder by now.

"Okay." Josh draws a deep breath. "Darryl, that one." He points to a slightly smaller juvenile rex directly below, then to a similar one. "Harry, that one. Aim to land on the shoulders and hook your heels in under the armpits, okay? Hook 'em in good. Try not to grab their crest feathers unless you really have to, it'll upset 'em more. And hang the prods from your backs while you jump so you don't drop 'em."

"Wha—"

Josh carries right on over Harry's protest. "Once the fence is down, zap your rex in the tail to get it moving. Try to stay on until we're out of sight of the camp, then slide down its back and off. Roll when you hit the ground, then stay completely still until they've run on their way. Okay?"

"Not even remotely okay," whispers Harry.

"Come on. *Hook in. Hang on.* Got it?" Josh swings his prod onto his back.

"Got it," I whisper, my mouth dry, arranging my prod's carry strap across my body.

"We *can't*—" protests Harry, though, like a sleep-walker, he's putting his own prod onto his back.

"This or a bullet," says Josh. "If you're lucky. Weigh the odds. Trust me, these are better. Let's go."

He grabs Harry's hand and I grab Harry's other hand, positioning him over the recommended juvenile. That puts me nicely over mine.

This is crazy. This is *crazy*.

This is our only chance.

"Three," says Josh. "Two, one, *jump...*"

HARRY

Josh jumps. Darryl jumps. I'm kinda surprised to find that I've jumped too.

The idea of landing on that bony backbone with my legs apart from that height is unthinkable, so I land on my bent knees, which works well until I almost bounce right off. Letting my legs slip quickly down the rex's sides, I sprawl forwards, desperately trying to grip. The last of its remaining juvenile plumage is thin and scraggly, and just when I think I'm gonna have to grab at its crest or slide all the way to the ground, my foot catches on the rex's forearm.

108

Quickly, I push myself back up onto the shoulders, getting my arms around the thick neck and trying to hook my heels securely under the armpits as the rex spins around, tossing its head and making confused sounds. I guess a wild one would completely lose it but I don't weigh much compared to it and this one's so used to humans it's not quite so freaked out. I'm able to stay on, just about. Ah, finally—heels in place.

I catch a glimpse of Josh settling himself on his juvenile's back as though he rides T. rex every day, and Darryl clinging wildly but seeming fairly secure. The next time around, I see Josh giving a rex that's facing the fence a good hard zap with his prod.

Zap. Zap.

By the time my rex turns around yet again, several roaring rex are charging towards the fence, full-tilt. They go straight through it. More roars as some of them get zapped. Guess they didn't even know what it was. They keep right on going, though. Fence is good and down, now.

"Come on!" Josh reaches back and gives his rex a tap with the prod.

Oh yeah, I need to do that too! I get hold of my prod and reach back, tensing all my leg muscles so I don't get left behind, like at the start of an orni race, then give my own rex a tap with the activated prod.

Whoa! It surges forward so fast I only just manage to throw myself forward and get a good grip again.

Without my heels hooked in I'd definitely have been off. As usual, Josh knew what he was talking about.

JOSHUA

I look back as my ride pounds through the hole in the fence, trying to keep my eyes on the others. Harry's rex is following. So is Darryl's, good.

No! At a lunge from a larger rex, Darryl's animal swerves away with a pack of smaller juveniles, heading back into the camp. *No, no, no!*

I crane my neck, following her progress for as long as I can—then we're out of sight. Unlike the she-rex in the egg barn, these juveniles are young, healthy, and well-muscled. Free to run for the first time in their cooped-up lives, they're really opening it up, nerves and excitement and the memory of the prods driving them on. We're out of sight of the camp already, and we need to dismount.

We're gotta get them to slow down, though. This would be like jumping from the turret of a fast-moving HabVi. Harry's staring at me, his face a pale oval in the moonlight. I hold up the prod so he can—hopefully—see it and imitate me, then reach forward to wave it near my rex's eyes. A basic form of steering.

Its head jerks to the left, and then we're pounding towards rougher ground where the valley side begins to rise. The less stable footing soon slows the rex down.

110

Like many carni'saurs that are solitary as full-grown adults, male juvenile rex form bachelor packs for safety, so I'm not surprised that a bunch of the others follow Harry and me onto this worse terrain. My rex is one of the larger ones, an obvious candidate for a pack leader.

Yep, they're slowing. We can try to get off soon. Preferably when we're at the back of the pack, though, where we won't get stepped on or eaten.

Uh-oh. No sooner has the full-out running slowed than the rex are snapping at one another again. We've just loosed a whole bunch of age groups together that have never interacted before and *their* priority is to establish a pecking order, not to allow the humans they don't even realize are here to dismount safely.

We really need to—

"Josh!"

Even as Harry yells, I sense the attack coming from my left. I have the prod up and over the back of the rex's neck, almost in position as the rex's open jaws come towards my shoulder. Too slow... The teeth sink into my flesh as I shove the prod into its mouth and activate it.

Its mouth flies open as it recoils from the pain, so that it barely drags at my flesh and leaves my shoulder and arm in place, for a wonder, though it still almost unseats me. With a deafening roar, it lumbers away.

My rex is smaller but I think I just promoted him to top position with that full-in-the-mouth zap. The stupid

111

thought drifts through my mind as I cling to the rex's back, gasping in pain. My left arm feels heavy, my muscles not wanting to work. Blood flows down my chest and back. My scentBlock is useless, now.

I'm a bloody, juicy snack at perfect nibbling height. I've gotta get off, *now*. I try to take a look around, judge my chances of being stepped on, but my vision blurs.

Off, Josh. Get off.

I loosen my grip on the rex's neck and free my heels. I intend to slide down its spine and off just before I'd end up hanging onto the tail, but my left arm won't grip at all and the rex turns abruptly, pitching me off sideways.

Falling...then, *argh!* Ribs crack as I land full on the electric prod, same side as the bite. I lie, gasping, winded. I can't see the rex, can't see...anything. Doesn't matter, I couldn't move right now even to avoid being stepped on. But the vibrations beneath me are reducing. The brand new bachelor pack is moving away. Far too well-fed to be interested in the blood smell, with this whole new world to explore.

Thanks, Saint Des.

"Josh? Josh?" Hands grip me, try to sit me up. I groan as pain knifes through me. "Josh, how badly are you hurt?"

"Winded. Give me...minute," I gasp.

"I *saw* it bite you. *Outage*, you're bleeding so much..."

And I broke my ribs. *Misfire*, but this ain't good. I try to force my mind into gear. Bleeding. Unarmed. The 'Vi is a mile up the mountainside. Camp full of very angry men. Darryl?

Move, Josh.

"Help me...sit up. *Argh...*"

Upright at last, I try to focus. The rex have run happily on their way. How many will Jason manage to round up? The far bigger danger, where *is* Jason? He'll be frantic to catch them—even ten unexpected rex popping up in a region will make DAPdep take a closer look, let alone *fifty*.

I peer back towards the camp—no sign of pursuit, yet. Odds are high none of the guys actually noticed us in the dark, flat against the rex's backs. That *misfiring* critter that bit me sure didn't—he was definitely going for my mount.

I glance down at my shoulder. My parka glistens damply in the dim moonlight. Too much blood. But we're completely exposed, here. If Jason drives into sight...

"Let's get into those crags," I tell Harry.

I try to stand and almost fall. Harry gets my good arm over his shoulder—*oh-heck-that-hurts!*—and helps me. I've never been so glad to collapse on a boulder. Gasping with pain.

"Clotter..." I manage, in-between gasps. "Gotta stop the bleeding. Use the flashlight..."

113

This crag is screening us from the camp well enough.

Bit by a short-circuiting *rex*. So many teeth. I'm in better shape than Dad, though, can't complain... "Help me get this coat off..."

Harry eases my parka off that arm, which ain't working properly. I can barely help and every movement stabs through my ribs and shoulder like a knife. I don't pass out from the pain—quite. My head fuzzes and echoes. I'm shivering even before the icy night air gets under my coat. But finally he's got enough access to pour the blood-clotting crystals into each wound. One by one. It takes a while.

"There...there are a lot of punctures," he says, his voice low and fearful. "But...I think the crystals are stopping the bleeding."

"Yeah," I try to sound confident. "It didn't get a chance to bite down. I'll be okay. Flesh wounds."

"Where's Darryl? I haven't seen her since the camp..."

"Her rex swerved and went the other way with another pack. I saw them take down the fence just before I lost line of sight and she was still on, then. She got out, Harry."

"Can we go find her?"

Go find her? I could laugh. I could weep. Exactly what I was planning when I was trying to scrape myself off the ground just now, but...

"We'd have to go past the camp or make a long diversion along the mountainside to get anywhere near where we last saw her. I'm not even a hundred percent sure I can make it up that mountain to the 'Vi. That's where she'll be heading so we're gonna have to meet her back there."

"But—"

"We're completely scent-compromised, Harry. I've lost a lot of blood and broken some ribs and have Saint Des only knows how many puncture wounds. We have to go straight back to the 'Vi."

"You broke your ribs too?" Dismay fills his voice.

"Fell from too high and landed on the prod."

"*Outage.*" Harry wipes at my shoulder some more, front and back. "Okay, I think the bleeding's stopped, are you good to go?"

No. I want to keep sitting here so it doesn't hurt so bad. But that ain't an option. Perhaps if we get back to the 'Vi quickly enough, we can do something to help Darryl. Not sure what, with my head this foggy. Something...

Harry eases the coat back onto me and zips it up carefully.

"Harry, take my frights." I doubt I could deploy 'em, right now. The thought of jerking anything... No.

Fumbling with the unfamiliar fastenings, he obeys, strapping them to his own arms. I let him try 'em while we were watching Jason's camp, so he knows how to use 'em. Then he helps me settle my left hand inside my breast pocket, as a makeshift sling, before supporting me to my feet. Heck, it hurts. A mile up a mountain, like this? I swallow.

"Harry, listen up a moment. If I start going into shock too badly I might get irrational. Might start wanting to sit down and not keep going. Go to sleep, even. You keep me moving, you understand, whatever I say?"

The moon's almost gone in again, but I catch the nervous glint of his eyes. "Sure. Of course."

"Okay. Let's go."

HARRY

Josh is shaking, still. He's already in shock, right, must be? "D'you want that blanket on?"

He shakes his head. "It'll reflect every tiny scrap of moonlight that comes through the clouds and make a racket. Let's just get back to the 'Vi quickly. If walking up this mountain don't warm me up, nothing will."

I carry one prod; he leans heavily on the other, digging it into the snow and shale. It's so steep, it's hard enough going for me, uninjured and with a free hand. The moon peeps out only now and then, so I clip the red flashlight to my shoulder, turned down to minimum, to give a tiny amount of illumination. There's no question of denning up and waiting for daylight, now.

I talk a little, on the easier stretches, to distract Josh from the pain. To try to. Very quietly. It's not hard—there are things I wanna know.

"Josh, who opened the pens? Was it you?"

"Sure."

"But you weren't touching the controls."

"Carni'saur pens have timers, Harry," he pants. "For safer handling. Set the timer. Back up a 'Vi or a trailer to the barn doors, make sure all temporary fencing is properly secure...and let the pens open without...having to compromise it to go back inside. When Caleb...got the drop on us...I just hit...one minute...instead of three hours."

"Three hours?"

"Yeah. If Jason don't fix that fence straight-off—and I bet he'll be too busy...trying to round up his stock—he's gonna lose his she-rex, too. Assuming he don't notice first."

You'll have to take your chances. He did let them out—kinda.

"Is Caleb dead?"

"Dunno. Don't much care."

Remembering the way he tried to feed me to the juveniles...yeah, I'm not sure I care much either.

"Better for us if he is," mutters Josh. "Unless Jason saw us leaving. Worst scenario, that would be."

"You, uh, don't feel bad?"

"A rex farmer who...runs from T. rex? Heck, that ain't hardly...my fault...if he did...get et. Anyway, him or us, Harry. Sure, I feel bad, but only about *this bad*."

He indicates what I suspect is a very small measurement indeed between his thumb and forefinger in the darkness, then stumbles onwards. "Not sure they did eat him, anyway," he mumbles. "Awful...quick and quiet...if they did. Might've hid."

He struggles to climb another steep slope. I have to take the prod for a moment to let him use his hand, giving him a push up with my shoulder. He groans slightly as he heaves himself to the top, but takes the prod back and continues without a word.

After thinking about what he just said for a while, I say, "So Jason's gonna know what we did?"

"Mebbe," Josh is panting too hard for long responses. I'm starting to feel mean making him talk.

"He'll kill us."

"If he...catches...us."

"We're gonna have to leave the state, aren't we? No choice, now. But..." My heart sinks into my belly like a box of ammo dropped into a pond. "That doesn't matter now, does it? I mean, Caleb simply couldn't *imagine* why we were there, you saw his face. And Jason heard a perfect description of our footprints and didn't even *think* of us three. These guys had nothing at all to do with Dad's kidnapping, did they?"

Josh stumbles on a loose patch of snow and falls to

118

one knee with a grunt of agony. Shakes his head tiredly before struggling back to his feet with some help from me. "I'm sorry, Harry. Jason talked big and bad and...it seemed like...our only lead. But you're right. This was a false trail."

We climb upwards in silence, on and on. Josh stops replying to my would-be motivational remarks, his head hanging, his breathing ragged. Where's Darryl? Is she okay? I clutch the prod as the darkness presses around me. With these prods, we're probably safer than we were on the way down—but I don't feel it. Darryl was here, then, Josh was alert and unhurt, and the excitement of thinking we might find Dad made predators seem a far-away threat.

Josh loses his footing and his injured shoulder slams into the slope ahead, dragging a smothered groan from his throat.

If you're hurt, don't make noise—don't sound like tasty prey. I can hear him saying it, but I dunno if I could do as well as he's doing.

He lies, panting, and there's a hint of a sob in his gasping breaths. How bad is he hurt? Flesh wounds, huh? But there were so *many* of them. So much blood...

I'm not even a hundred percent sure I can make it up that mountain to the 'Vi. Only now do his words register properly. The icy breath down my spine has nothing to do with the slight breeze that's rising.

"Josh?"

"M'o'kay." He struggles to his feet again with my assistance, but he doesn't move on immediately. "Harry, listen to me." He sounds as serious as I've ever heard him, his gloved hand gripping my arm.

"Yeah?"

"I'm bigger than you and you can't carry me. That's just a plain fact. If it gets to the point where I can't keep going, you leave me and get yourself back to the 'Vi. That's an order. Understand?"

Leave him? Oh sure, that would go down well with Darryl. Yeah, sis, I left Josh on the mountainside like so much carrion. How could I possibly *leave* him?

No point standing here arguing about it until something eats us, though. "Yeah, sure, Josh. I understand."

"Okay, let's go..." He stumbles onwards.

He's definitely hurt worse than he's letting on, if he's talking about me *leaving* him. *Saint Des, help us?*

Less than a mile to the 'Vi, and we'll be safe. Kinda. Just that massive bite in Josh's shoulder, Darryl's whereabouts, and a vengeful Jason to worry about.

And Dad. Who *wasn't down there*. Which means this was all for *nothing*. Josh hurt, Darryl missing...

Josh staggers, seeming ready to fall. I pull his arm over my shoulder, hauling him up the slope, step by step. I won't leave him. I won't!

We are gonna make it.

Somehow.

120

Don't miss unSPARKed 7:

FEAR

+

DID YOU MISS BOOKS 1-5?
PICK THEM UP TODAY!

 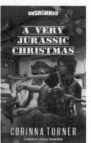

DON'T FORGET THE PREQUELS!

*The dragon roared, its jaws so close to Thane's head
that*

I waggled the page gently in the air, waiting for my writing to dry. One final, blank double spread remained. Good. I'd made the little book myself.

The ink was dry. I turned to that last page and found the place on the computer printout I was copying from...

he felt his eardrums burst. But the sword had done its work and, eviscerated, the beast began to topple.

Thane rolled frantically to his feet and ran. The huge body obliterated where he'd been lying, but Thane wasn't interested in that. He kept right on running to where Marigold was struggling to free herself.

"That's the last time I go riding without my spurs!" she told him. "I could've cut my way out of here by now..."

Thane ignored her grumbles. He couldn't hear properly anyway. He whipped out a dagger and freed her. "Marigold?" He could hardly hear himself. "Are you all right?"

"Oh, I'm fine. At least I had my rosary."

Thane thought of all the things he wanted to say to her. The way he felt about her, he wanted to do everything just right. Could he get down on one knee without losing his balance and would he be able to hear what she said in reply...?

Then Marigold's arms wrapped around him like vines around their supporting tree. And when she kissed him, he knew the answer to all his questions was a heartfelt,

'Yes.'

I wrote the last word with great care and put the lid on the pen. All done. I smiled as I pictured Bane reading the tale. *Where are the slain dragons? Where are the rescued maidens?* he would complain after reading my stories. Just this once, in this tale just for him, there were all the dragons he could desire. But only one maiden.

A funny way to declare your love, but I couldn't leave it unsaid. And if I *did* pass my Sorting...well, we were both eighteen, we'd be leaving school at the end of the year and would be free to register, so perhaps it was time we were finally honest with each other.

Picking up the printout of the story, I ripped it into small pieces and threw it in the bin, then closed the handwritten book, slipping it into the waterproof pouch I'd made for it. On my aged—but no less loved for that—laptop, I called up the file and pressed 'delete'. Bane's story was his alone.

The pouch went into my bag as I checked its contents again. Clothes, underwear, sewing things, my precious bookReader—filled to capacity—and what little else was permitted. No laptop, alas, and no rosary beads for Margaret in this all too real world. I touched the waterproof pouch—must warn Bane not to show the story around. A dangerous word had slipped in there, near the end. A little bit of myself.

The contents of the bag were all present and correct, as they'd been since last night. Zipping it up, I stood for a moment, looking around. This had been my room since I was born and how I wanted to believe I'd be back here this evening, unpacking my bag again. But I'd never been very good at fairy tales. Happy Ever After didn't happen in real life. Not while you were alive.

I kicked at my long purple skirt for a moment, then picked up my jacket and slipped it on. Sorting day was a home clothes day. No need for school uniform at the Facility. I was packed and ready—packed, anyway—and couldn't delay any longer. I put my bag over my shoulder and headed downstairs.

My parents were waiting in the hall. I almost wished they weren't. That they were off with Kyle—*gone*.

Mum's face was so pale. "Margo, you can't seriously intend to go today." Her voice was hoarse with desperation. "You know the chances of...of..."

"I know the chances of me passing are very small." With great effort I kept my voice from shaking. "But you know why I have to go."

"It's not too late..." Bleak hopelessness in Dad's voice. "The Underground would hide you..."

I had to get out of there. I had to get out before they wore down my resolve.

"It's too late to teach me to be selfish now," I snapped, switching automatically from Latin to English as I opened the front door and stepped out onto the step.

"Margo..."

I turned to meet Mum's embrace and I wanted to cling to her like a little girl, except that was how she was clinging to me. I stroked her hair and tried to comfort her. "It'll be all right, Mum, really," I whispered. "I might even pass, you know."

She released me at last, stepped back, mopping her eyes—trying to be strong for me. "Of course. You may pass. Keep the faith, darling." Her voice shook; right here, right now, she could hardly get the familiar words out.

"Keep the faith," said Dad, and his voice shook too.

I cupped my hand and made the Fish with finger and thumb, behind my bag so the neighbors couldn't see. "Keep the faith." It came out like an order. I blushed, smiled apologetically, took one last look at their faces and hurried down the steps.

The EuroBloc Genetics Department inspectors were waiting at the school gates to check off our names. I joined the line, looking into the boys' schoolyard for Bane. A hotel car pulled up and a white-faced woman helped a tall boy from the back seat—who was *he?* His hair was like autumn leaves... Oh. He held a long thin white cane with a soft ball on one end. Blind. My insides clenched in sympathy. What must it be like to have no hope at all?

"Name?" demanded the inspector on the boys' gate.

"Jonathan Revan," said the boy in a very cold, collected voice. "And wouldn't it be an awful lot simpler if my parents just dropped me at the Facility?"

The inspector looked furious as everyone sniggered their

125

appreciation at this show of courage.

"Name?" It was my turn. The blind boy was passing through the gates, his shoulders hunched now, as though to block the sound of the woman's weeping. A man was shepherding her back to the car.

"Margaret Verrall."

The woman marked off my name and jerked the pen towards the girls' yard. "In."

Inside, I headed straight for the wall between the schoolyards. Bane was there, his matte black hair waving slightly in the breeze. His mother used to keep it short, to hide its strangeness, but that'd only lasted 'til he was fast enough to outrun her. The inspector on the boys' gate was shooting a suspicious glance at him.

"Looking forward to being an adult?" Bane asked savagely, watching Jonathan Revan picking his way across the schoolyard, his stick waving sinuously in front of him. Something clicked.

"That's your friend from out at Little Hazleton, isn't it? The preKnown, who's never had to come to school?"

"Yeah." Bane's face was grim.

"Did you hear what he said to the inspector? He's got some nerve."

"He's got that, all right. Shame he can't see a thing."

"He'd have to see considerably *more* than a thing to pass."

"Yeah." Bane kicked the wall, scuffing his boots. "Yeah, well, I always knew there was nothing doing."

"It was nice of you to be friends with him."

Bane looked embarrassed and kicked the wall even harder. "Well, he's got a brain the size of the EuroBloc main server. He'd have been bored out of his mind with only the other preKnowns to talk to."

Oh no, perhaps I flattered myself, but...if Bane was preoccupied with Jonathan Revan...he really hadn't realized I was in danger! Although I'd always tried so hard not to let him figure it out part of me had assumed he knew by now. I mean, how could he not have *realized?* We'd known each other since, well, forever. He'd always been there, along with Mum and Dad, Kyle, Uncle Peter...

126

"Bane, I need to talk to you."

He looked around, his brown eyes surprised. He sat on the wall and rested his elbows on the railings. "Now? Not... after our Sorting?"

Were his thoughts running along the same lines as mine earlier? I sat down as well, which brought our faces very close. "Bane...it may not be very easy to talk...after."

His eyes narrowed. "What d'you mean?"

"Bane..." There was no easy way to say this. "Bane, I probably won't pass."

His face froze into incredulous disbelief—he really hadn't realized. He'd thought me Safe. *Bane, I'm so sorry.*

"You...of course you'll pass! You're as smart as Jon, you can keep the whole class spellbound, hanging on your every word..."

"But I can't do math to save my life."

There was a long, sick silence.

"Probably literally," I added, quite unnecessarily.

Bane remained silent. He saw the danger now. You only had to fail one single test. He looked at me at last and there was something strange in his eyes, something it took me a moment to recognize. Fear.

"Is it really *that* bad, your math?"

"It's almost non-existent," I said as gently as I could. "I have severe numerical dyslexia, you know that."

"I didn't realize. I just never..." There was guilt in his eyes, now; guilt that he'd gone through life so happy and confident in his physical and mental perfection that he'd never noticed the shadow hanging over me. "Didn't Fa... your Uncle Peter...teach you enough?"

"Uncle Peter managed to teach me more than anyone else ever has, but I'm actually not sure it's possible to teach me *enough.*"

"I just never thought..."

"Of course you didn't think about it. Who thinks about Sorting unnecessarily? Anyway, this is for you." I put the pouch into his hand. "Don't let anyone see it until you've read it; I don't think you'll want to flash it around."

His knuckles whitened around it. "Margo, what are you

doing here? If you think you're going to fail! Go, go now, I'll climb over and distract the inspector; the Underground will hide you..."

"Bane, stop, stop! I can't miss my Sorting, don't you understand? There was never any way I was going to get out of it—no one's allowed to leave the department with preSort age children and after today I'll show up as a SortEvader on every system in the EuroBloc..."

"So go underground!" He dropped his voice to a whisper. "You of all people could do that in an instant!"

"Yes, Bane, I could. And never mind spending the rest of my life running, can't you see why I, *of all people*, cannot run?"

He slammed his fist into the wall and blood sprung up on his knuckles. "This is because of the Underground stuff, isn't it? Your family are in too deep."

"Bane..." I captured his hand before he could injure it any more. "You know the only way the sanctuary will stay hidden is if the house *isn't* searched and if I run, what's the first thing they'll do?"

"Search your house."

"Search my house. Arrest my parents. Lay a trap for the next Underground members who come calling. Catch the priests when they come. You know what they do to the priests?"

"I know." His voice was so quiet I could hardly hear him.

"And you want that to happen to *Uncle* Peter? *Cousin* Mark? How can you suggest I *run?*"

He said nothing. Finally he muttered, "I wish you'd given this stuff up years ago..."

Bane had never understood my faith; he knew it would probably get me killed one day. He'd tried his hardest to talk me out of it before my sixteenth birthday, oh, how he'd tried. But he accepted it. He might not understand the faith angle, but getting killed doing something to wind up the EuroGov was right up his street.

The school bell began to ring and he looked up again, capturing my eyes. "I suppose then you wouldn't have been you," he murmured. "Look, if you don't pass..." his voice grew firmer, "if you don't pass, I'll have to see what I can do about it. Because...well...I've been counting on marrying you for a very long time, now, and I've no intention of letting anything stop me!"

My heart pounded—joy, but no surprise. How we felt about each other had been an unspoken secret for years. "Anything, such as the entire EuroBloc Genetics Department? Don't bite off more than you can chew, Bane."

He didn't answer. He just slipped an arm through the railings and snagged me, his lips coming down on mine. My arms slid through the railings, around his strong back, my lips melted against his and suddenly the world was a beautiful, beautiful place and this was the best day of my life.

We didn't break apart until the bell stopped ringing.

"Well," I whispered, looking into his brown eyes, "now I can be dismantled happily, anyway."

His face twisted in anguish. "Don't say that!" He kissed me again, fiercely. "Don't worry..." His hands cupped my face and his eyes glinted. "Whatever happens, *don't worry.* I love you and I *will not* leave you there, you understand?"

Planting one last kiss on my forehead, he swung his bag onto his shoulder and sprinted across the schoolyard, the pouch still clasped in his hand. I watched him go, then picked up my own bag and followed the last stragglers through the girls' door.

The classroom was unusually quiet, bags and small cases cluttering the aisles. Taking my place quickly, I glanced around. There were only two preKnowns in the class. Harriet looked sick and resigned, but Sarah didn't understand about her Sorting or the Facility or anything as complex as that. The known Borderlines were every shade of pale. The Safe looked sober but a little excited. The pre-Sorting ban on copulation would be gone tomorrow. No doubt the usual orgy would ensue.

Bane's last words stuck in my mind. I knew that glint in his eye. I should've urged him much more strenuously not to do anything rash. Not to put himself in danger. Now it was too late.

"I saw you and Bane," giggled Sue, beside me. "Jumping the gun a little, aren't you?"

"As if you haven't done any gun jumping yourself," I murmured. Sue just giggled even harder.

"Margy...? Margy...?"

"Hi, Sarah. Have you got your bag?"

Sarah nodded and patted the shabby bag beside her.

"They explained to you, right? That you'll be going on a sleep-over?"

Sarah nodded, beaming, and pointed at me. "Margy come too?"

"Perhaps. Only the most special children will be going, you know."

Sarah laughed happily. I swallowed bile and tried not to curse the stupid driver who'd knocked her down all those years ago and left her like this. Tried not to curse her parents, who'd put her into care, sued the driver for his Child Permittance so they could replace her, and promptly moved away.

"Children..." The deputy headmistress. She waited for quiet. "This is the last time I will address you as such. This is a very special day for you all. After your Sorting, you will be legally adults."

Except those of us who would scarcely any longer count as human. She didn't mention that bit.

"Now, do your best, all of you. Doctor Vidran is here from the EGD to oversee your Sorting. Over to you, Doctor Vidran..."

Doctor Vidran gave a long and horrible speech about the numerous benefits Sorting brought to the human race. By the time he'd finished I was battling a powerful urge to go up and shove his laser pointer down his throat. I managed to stay in my seat and concentrated on trying to love this misguided specimen of humanity, to forgive him his part in what was probably going to happen to me. It was very difficult.

"...A few of you will of course have to be reAssigned, and it is important that we always remember the immense contribution the reAssigned make, in their own way..."

Finally he shut up and bade us turn our attention to our flickery desk screens for the Intellectual Tests. My happiness at his silence took me through Esperanto, English, Geography, History, ComputerScience, Biology, Chemistry and Physics without hitch, but then came Math. I tried. I really, really tried. I tried until I thought my brain would explode and then I thought about Bane and my parents and I tried some more. But it was no good. No motivation on earth could enable me to do most of those sums without a calculator. I'd failed.

The knowledge was a cold, hard certainty in the pit of my stomach all the way through the Physical Tests after a silent, supervised lunch. I passed all those, of course. Sight, Hearing, Physiognomy and so on, all well within the acceptable levels. What about Jonathan Revan, a preKnown if ever there was one? Smart, Bane said, really smart, and Bane was pretty bright himself. Much good it'd do Jonathan. Much good it'd do me.

We filed into the gym when it was all over, sitting on benches along the wall. Bane guided Jonathan Revan to a free spot over on the boys' side. In the hall through the double doors the rest of the school fidgeted and chatted. Once the end of semester assembly was over, they were free for four whole weeks.

Free. Would I ever be free again?

I'd soon know. One of the inspectors was wedging the doors open as the headmaster took his place on the stage. His voice echoed into the gym. "And now we must congratulate our New Adults! Put your hands together, everyone!"

Dutiful clapping from the hall. Doctor Vidran stood by the door, clipboard in hand, and began to read names. A boy. A girl. A boy. A girl. Sorry, a young man, a young woman. Each New Adult got up and went through to take their seat in the hall. Was there a pattern...? No, randomized. Impossible to know if they'd passed your name or not.

My stomach churned wildly now. Swallowing hard, I stared across the gym at Bane. Jonathan sat beside him, looking cool as a cucumber, if a little determinedly so. *He* wasn't in any suspense. Bane stared back at me, his face grim and his eyes fierce. I drank in the harsh lines of his face, trying to carve every beloved detail into my mind.

"They might call my name," Caroline was whispering to Harriet. "They might. It's still possible. Still possible..."

Over half the class had gone through.

Still possible, still possible, they might, they might call my name... My mind took up Caroline's litany, and my desperate longing came close to an *ache*.

"Blake Marsden."

A knot of anxiety inside me loosened abruptly— immediately replaced by a more selfish pain. Bane glared at Doctor Vidran and didn't move from his seat. Red-faced, the deputy headmistress murmured in Doctor Vidran's ear.

Doctor Vidran looked exasperated. "Blake Marsden, known as Bane Marsden."

Clearly the best Bane was going to get. He gripped Jonathan's shoulder and muttered something, probably *bye*. Jonathan found Bane's hand and squeezed and said something back. Something like *thanks for everything*.

Bane shrugged this off and got up as the impatient inspectors approached him. *No...don't go, please...* Yes! He was heading straight for me—but the inspectors cut him off.

"Come on...Bane, is it? *Congratulations*, through you go..." Bane resisted being herded and the inspector's voice took on a definite warning note. "Now, you're an adult, it's your big day, don't spoil it."

"I just want to speak to..."

They caught his arms. He wrenched, trying to pull free, but they were strong men and there were two of them.

"You *know* no contact is allowed at this point. I'm sure your girlfriend will be through in a moment."

"Fiancée," snarled Bane, and warmth exploded in my stomach, chasing a little of the chill fear from my body. He'd read my story already.

"*If*, of course, your *fiancée*," Doctor Vidran sneered the un-PC word from over by the door, "is a perfect specimen. If not, you're better off without her, *aren't* you?"

Bane's nostrils flared, his jaw went rigid and his knuckles

clenched until I thought his bones would pop from his skin. Shoulders shaking, he allowed the inspectors to bundle him across the gym towards Doctor Vidran. *Uh oh...*

But by the time they reached the doors he'd got sufficient hold of himself he just stopped and looked back at me instead of driving his fist into Doctor Vidran's smug face. He seemed a long way away. But he'd never been going to reach me, had he?

"Love you..." he mouthed.

"Love you..." I mouthed back, my throat too tight for actual words.

Then a third inspector joined the other two and they shoved him through into the hall. And he was gone.

Gone. I might never see him again. I swallowed hard and clenched my fists, fighting a foolish frantic urge to rush across the gym after him.

"*Really,*" one inspector was tutting, "we don't usually have to drag them *that* way!"

"Going to end up on a gurney, that one," apologized the deputy headmistress, "So sorry about that..."

Doctor Vidran dismissed Bane with a wave of his pen and went on with the list.

"They might..." whispered Caroline, "they might..."

They might...they might...I might be joining Bane. I might... Please...

But they didn't. Doctor Vidran stopped reading, straightened the pages on his clipboard and glanced at the other inspectors. "Take them away," he ordered.

He and the deputy headmistress swung round and went into the hall as though those of us left had ceased to exist. As we kind of had. The only decent thing to do about reAssignees was to forget them. Everyone knew that.

One of the inspectors took the wedges from under the doors and closed them. Turned the key, locking us apart.

My head rang. I'd thought I'd known, I'd thought I'd been quite certain, but still the knowledge hit me like a bucket of ice-cold water, echoing in my head. Margaret Verrall. My name. They'd not called it. The last tiny flame of hope died inside me and it was more painful than I'd expected.

One of the boys on the bench opposite—Andrew Plateley—started crying in big, shuddering gasps, like he couldn't quite believe it. Harriet was hugging Caroline and Sarah was tugging her sleeve and asking what was wrong. My limbs felt heavy and numb, like they weren't part of me.

Doctor Vidran's voice came to us from the hall, just audible. "Congratulations, adults! What a day for you all! You are now free to apply for breeding registration, providing your gene scans are found to be compatible. I imagine your head teacher would prefer you to wait until after your exams next semester, though!"

The school laughed half-heartedly, busy sneaking involuntary glances to see who was left in the gym—until an Inspector yanked the blinds down over the door windows. Everyone would be glad to have us out of sight so they could start celebrating.

"After successful registration," the Doctor's cheerful voice went on, "you may have your contraceptive implants temporarily removed. The current child permittance is one child per person, so each couple may have two. Additional child permittances can be bought; the price set by the EGD is currently three hundred thousand Eurons, so I don't imagine any of you need to worry about that."

More nervous laughter from the hall. Normal life was through there. Exams, jobs, registering, having children, growing old with Bane...but I wasn't in there with him. I was out here. My stomach fluttered sickly.

"ReAssignees, up you get, pick up your bags," ordered one of the inspectors.

I got to my feet slowly and picked up my bag with shaking hands. Why did I feel so shocked? Had some deluded part of me believed this couldn't really happen? Around me everyone moved as though in a daze, except Andrew Plateley who just sat, rocking to and fro, sobbing. Jonathan said something quietly to him but he didn't seem to hear.

The inspector shook Andrew's shoulder, saying loudly, "Up." He pointed to the external doors at the other end of the gym but Andrew leapt to his feet and bolted for the hall. He yanked at the doors with all his strength, sobbing, but they just rattled slightly under his assault and remained solidly closed. The inspectors grabbed him and began to drag him away, kicking and screaming. There was a sudden, suffocating silence from beyond those doors, as everyone tried not to hear his terror.

Doctor Vidran's voice rushed on, falsely light-hearted, "And I'm *sure* I don't need to remind you that you can only register with a person of your own ethnicity. Genetic mixes are, *of course*, not tolerated and all such offspring will be destroyed. And as you know, all unregistered children automatically count as reAssignees from birth, but I'm sure you're all going to register correctly so none of you need to worry about anything like that."

They'd got Andrew outside and the inspectors were urging the rest of us after him. It seemed a terribly long way, my bag seemed to weigh a very great deal and I still felt sick. I swallowed again, my hand curving briefly, unseen, into the Fish. Be strong.

"And that's all from me, though your headmaster has kindly invited me to stay for your end of semester presentations. Once again, congratulations! Let's hear it for Salperton's New Adults!"

The school whooped and cheered heartily behind us. A wave of crazy, reality-defying desperation swept over me— this must be how Andrew had felt. As though, if I could just get into that hall, *I'd* have the rest of my life ahead of me too...

Reality waited outside in the form of a little EGD minibus. Imagine a police riot van that mated with a tank. Reinforced metal all over, with grilles over the windows. Reaching the hall would achieve precisely *nothing*. So *get a grip, Margo*.

I steadied Sarah as she scrambled into the minibus and passed my bag up to her. She busied herself lifting my bag and hers onto the overhead luggage racks, beaming with pride at her initiative.

"Thanks, Sarah." A soft white ball wandered into my vision—there was Jonathan Revan, the last left to get in after me. I almost offered help, then thought better of it.

135

"Jonathan, isn't it? Just give a shout if you want a hand."

"Thanks, Margaret." His eyes stared rather eerily into the minibus. Or rather, through the minibus, for they focused not at all. "I'm fine."

His stick came to rest against the bus's bumper and his other hand reached out, tracing the shape of the seats on each side, then checking for obstructions at head height. Just as the EGD inspectors moved to shove him in, he stepped up into the bus with surprising grace. I climbed in after him just as the school fire alarms went off, the sound immediately muffled by the inspectors slamming the doors behind me.

"Bag?" Sarah was saying to Jonathan, holding out her hand.

"Sorry?"

"Bag," I told him. "Would you like her to put your bag up?"

"Oh. Yes, thank you. What's your name?"

"Sarah."

"Sarah. Thanks."

Bet he wouldn't have let me put his bag up for him! Sarah sat down beside Harriet, so I took a seat next to Jonathan. The first pupils were spilling out into the schoolyards and I craned my neck to try and catch a glimpse of Bane. A last glimpse.

"Any guesses who set that off?" said Jonathan dryly.

"Don't know how he'd have done it, but yeah, I bet he did."

The minibus began to move, heading for the gates, and I twisted to look out the rear window, through the bars. Nothing...

We pulled onto the road and finally there he was, streaking across the schoolyard to skid to a halt in front of the gates just as they slid closed. Bane gripped them as though he wanted to shake them, rip them off their hinges or throw them open...

The minibus went around a corner and he was gone.

Get I AM MARGARET today!

136

ABOUT THE AUTHOR

Corinna Turner has been writing since she was fourteen and likes strong protagonists with plenty of integrity. Although she spends as much time as possible writing, she cannot keep up with the flow of ideas, for which she offers thanks—and occasional grumbles!—to the Holy Spirit. She is the author of over twenty-five books, including the Carnegie Medal Nominated I Am Margaret series, and her work has been translated into four languages. She was awarded the St. Katherine Drexel award in 2022.

She is a Lay Dominican with an MA in English from Oxford University and lives in the UK. She is a member of a number of organizations, including the Society of Authors, Catholic Teen Books, Catholic Reads, the Angelic Warfare Confraternity, and the Sodality of the Blessed Sacrament. She used to have a Giant African Land Snail, Peter, with a 6½" long shell, but now makes do with a cactus and a campervan.

Get in touch with Corinna...

Facebook: Corinna Turner

Twitter: @CorinnaTAuthor

Don't forget to sign up for

NEWS
&
FREE SHORT STORIES
at:

www.UnSeenBooks.com

All Free/Exclusive content subject to availability.

Made in United States
Troutdale, OR
02/21/2024

17856766R00087